# JADA JOHNSON,
## INTERNATIONAL GIRL DETECTIVE

# JADA JOHNSON,
## INTERNATIONAL GIRL DETECTIVE

*The Case Of The Emperor's Scepter*

Carris Kane

| Library of Congress Control Number: | | 2021916316 |
| --- | --- | --- |
| ISBN: | Hardcover | 978-1-6641-8915-7 |
| | Softcover | 978-1-6641-8914-0 |
| | eBook | 978-1-6641-8913-3 |

Print information available on the last page.

Rev. date: 09/03/2021

**To order additional copies of this book, contact:**
Xlibris
844-714-8691
www.Xlibris.com
Orders@Xlibris.com
831257

# CHAPTER 1

Jada Johnson presented her boarding pass to the flight attendant and turned left aboard Air Italia 9410, direct flight to Rome, Italy. "Row 6, seats C, D, E, and F," her dad called out to Jada, who was in the lead ahead of him, her mom, and her brother, Justin. She stopped at the luxury cubicle that would be her home for the night. Jada and her family usually flew first class when they traveled with her dad, but it never got old. Jada plopped her backpack in the overhead compartment, then sank into the plush leather seat. She placed the fluffy white pillow in its crisp linen cover behind her head and cocooned herself against the air-conditioned chill of the cabin under the beige comforter embossed with the airline logo. She pushed a button in the armrest, turning on the massage function of the chair, and after a second's delay, felt a kneading sensation up and down her spine. Justin sat next to her and immediately reclined his seat into a flat bed. He grabbed the remote and started flipping through the in-flight entertainment system to choose the video games he would play and the movies he would watch on his personal TV screen.

At fourteen, Jada was already an experienced traveler. Whenever possible, Jada's parents took her and Justin with them on their trips abroad for work. Mrs. Johnson was the director of an international charity, and Mr. Johnson was an international businessman. Mr. Johnson was working on the purchase of an Italian company by the American corporation that he worked for. Negotiations of the deal were taking place in Rome during summer vacation, so Jada and Justin got to go with their parents on a two-week trip to the Eternal City. Jada always loved to travel, but she was particularly excited to go to Rome because there was a museum exhibit of a two-thousand-year-old artifact she had written a report on for her social studies class. She would actually get to see the ancient scepter of Emperor Maxentius that had recently been found in an archeological dig in Rome.

At the touch of a button, Justin rolled down the opaque divider between his seat and Jada's. "J, you hungry?" Justin offered Jada one of the protein bars he was always munching on. Two years older than Jada, he had shot up past her in height only in the past year and was working on filling out his 6'1" frame.

"Nah, J, I'm good," Jada responded, using the same nickname for Justin that he used for her. "I'll wait for the snack they are going to serve when we get up in the air."

As Jada watched the flight attendant make her rounds serving welcome beverages before takeoff—water, orange juice, and for the adults, champagne—she noticed a man who had been sitting near her family in the airport business lounge board the plane. He was dressed like a businessman in a dark suit and a white shirt, but Jada was surprised to note the dark edges of a wide tattoo on his neck that was not quite hidden by his collar. His thick, muscular build made the fabric of the business suit stretch tightly across his biceps and quadriceps, and the button strain to keep the jacket shut. He had longish hair slicked back with gel and a beard of dark stubble that did little to disguise a long scar down his left cheek, along which hair refused to grow. He looked more like a pro boxer cleaned up for a press conference than an executive on a business trip.

The large man lifted the heavy-looking metal case he was carrying as if it were a feather, put it in the overhead locker, and took the seat across the aisle and one row in front of Jada. As soon as he sat down he took out his cell phone, and spoke into it with his hand covering the mouthpiece. It was if as he didn't want his conversation heard *or* his lips read. Jada strained to hear what he was saying, but she realized the muffled talk was in another language. A sharp "*Da! Da!*" before he hung up was all she could make out. *Russian? Another Slavic tongue?* Jada wondered.

Jada needed to chew gum during takeoff and landing or else her ears would get stopped up from the change in air pressure. She realized that her gum was still in her backpack, so she stood up, got the gum out, then put the backpack back into the overhead compartment above her seat. In addition to gum, her backpack contained:

- her iPhone
- a guidebook on Rome
- hand lotion
- lip balm
- tissues
- her favorite fuzzy socks
- a pair of underpants and a T-shirt in case her checked luggage got lost
- a notebook
- a pen
- her passport
- her wallet
- a brush and a hairband to tame her hair before getting off the plane

She usually carried a Swiss Army knife, but she had to put it in her checked bag because sharp objects were not allowed in the cabin of the plane for security reasons.

As Jada arranged her thick, coffee-colored, shoulder-length tresses into a topknot for the flight, her eyes locked with the eyes of the muscle-bound "businessman," who was openly staring at her from his rear-facing seat. His steely gaze creeped her out, but she returned his stare until he looked away first. She sat back in her seat and let the roar of the engine, and the acceleration of the massive jumbo jet as it took off down the runway and lifted into the air, turn her thoughts to the thrill of flight and the anticipation of seeing a new country.

A few hours later, Jada finished watching a second movie. The cabin lights were dim, and most passengers were sleeping. She decided it was time for a nap, but first, a bathroom break. Justin was snoring softly in the seat/bed next to hers, and Jada carefully climbed over him to get to the aisle. Across the aisle, her parents were sleeping too. Jada noticed that part of the strap of her backpack was sticking out of the overhead compartment and made a mental note to put it fully inside on her return from the bathroom. To her surprise, when she came back to her seat, there was no sign of the strap sticking out. She opened the compartment to check if her backpack was still there. It was. *A flight attendant must have noticed the protruding strap and fixed it,* she decided, and pushing the thought to the back of her mind, settled down to sleep.

Six hours later, the Johnsons arrived at Fiumicino, Rome's airport, to a bright, sun-soaked morning. There were long lines at passport control, and the luggage belt spun empty for what seemed like hours before their baggage appeared. Jada's father led them through the green "Nothing to Declare" exit, but as they were passing through, a customs agent in a blue uniform came up to Justin and asked sharply, *"Da dov'e vieni?* Where are you coming from?"

"The United States," Justin replied. The officer motioned him over to a counter, and the rest of the Johnson family followed. Border officials at airports had the right to search the belongings of people entering their country to check if they were carrying anything illegal. They were usually searching for drugs. The customs officer began searching Justin's bags and motioned for Jada to put her backpack onto the counter as well. Jada's father, frowning, asked in Italian, "Is there a problem, Officer? We have a car waiting, and I have a meeting to attend. I'm here on business, and my family is joining me."

The officer looked up from his search, eyebrows raised, clearly surprised that the American spoke Italian. He zipped up Justin's suitcase and was about to let them go, when he hesitated, seemed to change his mind, opened Jada's backpack and peered inside. "Aha!" he cried as he pulled something out. *"Che cosa abbiamo qui!?* What do we have here?" They all stared at the object in the palm of his hand. It was a smooth eggshell-colored, ovoid-shaped carved figurine about four inches tall. A solid ivory egg Jada had never seen before and certainly had not packed in her bag. "Do you know that the importation of ivory is illegal in the European Union, *signorina*? It is a crime punishable by deportation or prison," the officer said menacingly to Jada. "Come with me." Over her parents' and Justin's objections, he took Jada firmly by the arm and led her away.

# CHAPTER 2

"Please sit," the customs officer said in a tone more command than offer, and pointed to a chair on the other side of a small table in a tiny room. Then he left, the door clicking shut behind him.

Jada had learned in her environmental studies class that thousands of elephants were cruelly and illegally slaughtered in Africa each year for their valuable tusks. There was a black market in ivory jewelry and figurines, as well as ground-up ivory powder, believed in some cultures to be a powerful medicine. She also knew that she had never seen the figurine before and had certainly not tried to smuggle it into Italy. The question was, who in the world would plant it on her and why?

Her heart hammered inside her chest. What if the customs officials denied her entry into Italy? What if they sent her and her entire family back to the US and her father's business plans were ruined? What if they threw her in an Italian jail for illegal smuggling?

Jada looked around the small windowless room for a clock, but the walls were bare. The officer had confiscated her backpack, so Jada didn't have her phone. Though she had done nothing wrong, paradoxically, Jada's palms started to sweat while her mouth went dry. She got up and tried the door, but the knob wouldn't turn. Jada suffered from claustrophobia, and she fought the sensation that the walls of the room were closing in on her. She paced around the table for a few minutes, then forced herself to sit down again. She knew that in order to extricate herself from this situation, she had to keep a cool head. She decided to breathe deeply and count to one hundred. Just as she got to ninety-eight and was about to get up and bang on the door to demand to be released, the doorknob turned and the door swung open. The customs officer was back, and he brought a friend. The two uniformed officers sat down across from Jada, and both stared at her coldly. The new guy—who was actually a woman twice the size of the first guy—cracked her knuckles, then folded her muscular arms across her chest. Jada decided to take the initiative and speak first. "*Signori*, the ivory is not mine. I did not bring it here. I have no idea how it got in my backpack." Despite her pounding heart, Jada looked the officers in the eyes and spoke clearly and slowly, hoping the second officer's English was good enough for her to understand, and more importantly, that they would both believe her.

Jada explained again that her dad was in Rome on business, their family was joining him as a vacation, and they had no connections with African ivory smugglers. She told them that the only explanation for her having the ivory was that her backpack had been tampered with on the plane. "My dad is here to meet with Augusto Boroni of Industria Boroni. This is the reason we are in Rome." Upon hearing the name Augusto Boroni, the customs officers, who had fixed their gaze on Jada with suspicion, quickly glanced at each other, then whispered back and forth before turning back to her. Noting their response, Jada decided to emphasize the connection with Boroni and continued, "Ask my dad for his business card. Call Signor Boroni's office to confirm their relationship."

"Your father is a business associate of Augusto Boroni?" the first customs officer asked. "*Un momento.*" He left the room, and Jada and the brawny second officer sat in awkward silence, awaiting his return. He came back shortly accompanied by yet another officer— their superior, judging from her demeanor. A brief conversation among the three agents ensued. There was much gesturing and whispering. Jada frowned in concentration as she tried to decipher what they were saying about her in Italian. She distinctly made out the name Boroni repeated several times.

At last the superior officer turned to Jada. "As your father is here on business with one of Italy's most important companies, headed by a most important family, we will not delay you any longer, *signorina*," she said. She opened the door for Jada, and escorted her back to her family in the customs area. Jada's mother rushed to embrace her as if she had just been released from a thirty-year jail term rather than a thirty-minute interrogation. Her father gave the officers a tongue-lashing about the inappropriateness of separating a minor from her family for questioning. He began to threaten a lawsuit, when Mrs. Johnson put her hand on his arm to calm him.

"We are most sorry for any inconvenience," the superior officer said to Mr. and Mrs. Johnson. "We take such matters very seriously, but we accept your daughter's explanation. Again, you have our sincerest apologies. We will, however, be retaining the ivory as it is contraband. *Benvenuti a Roma*," she finished, handing Jada her backpack. "Welcome to Rome."

*Clearly, the Boroni name carries weight in Italy,* Jada thought as they finally left customs and handed their luggage over to the driver who had come to pick them up. The customs agents had freed her and let them into the country after hearing that her father had dealings with Boroni. But it was also clear to Jada that someone did not want them in Italy. The ivory in her backpack was no accident. Someone had deliberately placed it there to try to stop them from entering the country, and she was determined to find out who was responsible.

# CHAPTER 3

Jada, Justin, and their mother entered their suite at the Hotel Eden, one of Rome's most luxurious hotels, exhausted but excited to be in a new country. Mr. Johnson had gone to his meeting. "Let's put the unpleasantness of our airport experience behind us," Mrs. Johnson said.

"Whoa, check out this place," Justin exclaimed. "I'm gonna enjoy staying here." The suite had a living room, a larger bedroom for Jada's parents, and two additional smaller bedrooms. There were two marble bathrooms as well. The decor was ornate, with antique furniture, oriental rugs, and brocade curtains. The style was Old-World luxury with ultramodern amenities. Jada was mentally preparing to argue with Justin over who would get the bedroom with the balcony and the stunning view of Rome and who would get the interior bedroom with no view, when he surprised her by announcing that he would take the interior room. "My own TV," he grinned, and turned on the huge flat screen on the wall opposite the bed. "Near the minibar as well," he said, grabbing a chocolate bar and a bottle of juice from the small fridge just outside his door. That suited Jada just fine, and she took her things into the pretty bedroom with a view and started to unpack.

"Don't ruin your appetite," Mrs. Johnson scolded Justin. "We are going to freshen up and then head out to walk around a bit and have lunch." Just then Mrs. Johnson spied a huge vase of flowers on a side table. She opened a card in a cream-colored envelope. "The flowers are from Augusto Boroni. And here's the invitation to that exhibit you wanted to see, Jada. *Please join us at a private reception for the unveiling of the Scepter of Emperor Maxentius.'* It's tonight at seven at the Rome Museum of Art and Antiquities. Let me text your dad and see if he'll be free in time. Jada, you wrote a report on him, didn't you? Who was Emperor Maxentius?" she asked, reaching into her handbag for her cell phone.

"You may not remember him from history class, Mom, since he ruled for only six years, from AD 306 to 312," Jada said. "A scepter is a long rod or staff made of ivory or a precious metal and topped with an orb or other ornament. It was a symbol of power and military might. Maxentius' scepter is a really big deal since it is the *only* Roman emperor's scepter ever found," she continued. "Emperors were often described in writing or depicted in art carrying a scepter. But until now, no one in modern times has ever seen an actual Roman emperor's scepter."

Justin had jumped onto his laptop to Google Emperor Maxentius. "Apparently, Maxentius wasn't such a great ruler," Justin added. "It says here that he was known for his vices and incompetence. He drowned in the Tiber River during a battle against another Roman emperor, Constantine, who then became sole ruler of the Roman Empire. Sounds like this scepter is something we should see."

"I agree," responded Mrs. Johnson. Just then her phone pinged. "Your dad says he'll meet us at the reception. Looks like we'll all get to see this rare artifact."

* * * * * * * *

That evening, Jada arrived at the reception a little groggy after a nap, but she was wide-eyed immediately upon walking into the entry hall of the museum. In the center of the room was a large rectangular box about six feet high and three feet across, sheathed in a red velvet curtain. At one corner was a yellow braided rope attached to the top of the curtain. A huge chandelier hung from the ceiling high above the box and cast light on the stunning antiquities surrounding the room. Tile mosaics lined the walls, and marble sculptures depicting ancient Roman and Greek heroes and heroines stood imposingly around the room.

The guests at the reception were as colorful and interesting as the art. Women in fashionable clothing with sleek hairdos tottered in sky-high heels and chatted with well-groomed and equally stylish men. Waiters in black tuxedos circulated the room, serving canapés and champagne to the adults and *aranciata*, orange soda, to the kids in attendance. A quartet of musicians played lively classical music, and Jada wouldn't have been surprised if the guests had paired up and started to waltz, such was the festive yet elegant atmosphere of the reception.

Jada scanned the room, people watching as much as appreciating the art, and she was startled to see a familiar face in the crowd. Standing near the center of the room, just a couple of feet from the curtained box, was the scarred, tattooed man from the plane. He was standing on the edge of a cluster of other guests, but Jada noticed that he wasn't really talking with them. In fact, he seemed quite distracted and kept glancing over at the curtain behind him. Jada suspected that he had something to do with the ivory in her backpack at the airport; she wasn't sure how, but she planned to find out before the evening was over.

Mr. Johnson found his family in the crowded room. "There you are," he said. "I have someone I want you to meet." He introduced a patrician white-haired man, elegantly dressed in an expensive-looking dark suit, light blue shirt, with a silk ascot around his neck. "Signor Augusto Boroni, head of Industria Boroni. This is my wife, Jocelyn; our son, Justin; and our daughter, Jada."

"Call me Augusto. *Molto piacere*, very pleased to meet you," Augusto said, bowing politely and kissing Mrs. Johnson's hand with a flourish. He shook Justin's hand, then turned to Jada. "*Che bella ragazza*! What a beautiful girl!" he commented, bending to kiss Jada's hand as well. "It is clear that, as you say, the apple does not fall far from the tree," he said, managing to compliment both Jada and Mrs. Johnson at the same time. Ordinarily, Jada knew, her mom would find such comments sexist and completely inappropriate, but she seemed utterly charmed by Augusto Boroni and smiled graciously at him.

"You must meet my grandson," he said to Jada. "He is a little shy around beautiful girls, but I'm sure you will like him. *Eccolo*, Carlo!

*Vieni qui!* Come here!" he beckoned to a tall, thin boy of about fifteen. Carlo Boroni had deep brown eyes, wavy black hair, and a calm yet confident manner. He was dressed in khaki pants, an Oxford shirt, and a light-weight cashmere sweater. "Where is your father, Carlo? I want him to meet Mr. Johnson and his family."

Carlo looked a bit uncomfortable. "Um, *Nonno*, he asked me to tell you that he had another engagement and wouldn't be able to make it tonight." Augusto pursed his lips in annoyance, but said nothing more about his son.

"James, Jocelyn, if you would please excuse me," Augusto Boroni said to Mr. and Mrs. Johnson with a slight bow, "I see the head of the Boroni Research and Development Department over there, and I need to have a quick word with him." He nodded toward an awkward man in a rumpled suit who was standing alone in a corner of the room sipping a drink self-consciously. "Carlo, take our young American guests around to have a closer look at the works of art. We have some time until the unveiling," he said with a smile.

Jada and Justin headed off with Carlo to walk around the exhibition hall. Justin became transfixed by a famous sculpture that he had learned about in art class, so Jada and Carlo left him circling the statue, examining it and taking photos. They chatted amiably and quickly discovered they shared a love of basketball, and that Carlo was as much of an NBA fan as Jada. "Do you watch the games online?" Jada asked.

"They are televised here, but because we are six hours ahead of US East Coast time, I usually record games and then watch the next day," Carlo responded. "But I watch the playoffs and championship games live."

"You stay up until four or five in the morning to watch basketball?" Jada asked, impressed with his dedication to the sport.

"Wouldn't you?" he replied with a smile. Jada had to admit that she would.

"Your English is really good," Jada commented. "You don't really have an accent."

"Thanks," Carlo replied. "My mother was American. She died when I was eight, but I learned English and got my accent from her."

"I'm sorry," Jada said, not knowing if it was the right thing to say.

"Thanks," Carlo replied simply, smiling his warm smile again, and Jada knew that it was.

As they strolled around the hall, Jada caught another glimpse of the tattooed man, and decided she had to approach him. He was someone she would not want to encounter in a dark alley, but she figured she'd be safe in a room full of people. He was not likely to admit to planting the ivory in her backpack, but she wanted to observe his reaction to her question. *Now or never,* she thought, and turned to ask Carlo to excuse her for a moment. When she turned back, the man had disappeared. Jada scanned the room and finally caught sight of him again at the end of the exhibition hall. His back was to her as he slipped through the doorway to another room of the museum. Jada pushed her way through the crowd of reception guests to the door through which the mysterious man had disappeared. She turned the handle. It was locked. "May I help you, *signorina?*" a museum guard asked, appearing from out of nowhere.

"I was just looking for someone," she said. "He left through this door."

"Impossible," replied the guard, shaking his head. "The other halls are closed this evening. This door has been locked since the museum closed to the public at 5:00 p.m."

"But I just saw him. He went through here a minute ago," Jada insisted.

"Are you implying that I am not doing my job?" the guard asked indignantly. Before Jada could respond, the music stopped and the clinking of a silver pen against a crystal glass rang out.

"*Signore* and *signori,* may I have your attention please. My name is Teresa Fabbri, and I am the director of the Rome Museum of Art and Antiquities. My assistant director, Marco Vitti, and I want to welcome you to tonight's exhibit. We are pleased and honored to have our museum patrons, the Boroni family, as well as so many international guests here tonight. It is my pleasure to invite you, our illustrious guests, to be the first to witness the unveiling of one of the most important archeological finds of the twenty-first century! Without further ado . . ."

She paused and a drumroll commenced from the musicians in the corner. "I bring to you . . ." The drumming intensified. "The Scepter of Emperor Maxentius!" Cymbals crashed as she pulled the braided rope and the velvet curtain fell to reveal . . . an empty glass case.

# CHAPTER 4

There was a collective gasp, followed by murmurs of disbelief as two hundred pairs of eyes stared at the transparent box that should have held an ancient scepter. Someone in the crowd laughed, thinking the situation was a joke, but the frantic cries of the museum director made clear that this was no laughing matter. "Guards!" she yelled. "Close the front exit! No one can leave until the authorities arrive." The guard standing next to Jada sprang into action, as did another guard across the room. They closed the two heavy front doors of the museum and stood blocking them. The director shouted into her cell phone, presumably talking to the police. Jada, meanwhile, was thinking that she had to get through the locked door leading to the other exhibition rooms. It might have been the thief's escape route.

Carlo appeared at her side. "Can you believe the scepter is gone? An object worth millions of euros just vanished into thin air."

"I need to get this door open," Jada said to him. "I saw someone sneak through it before the unveiling, and I think he might have something to do with the theft."

"I know another way around," Carlo replied. "My grandfather is a trustee of the museum. I did an internship here last summer. There is a small door for employees over there. It leads to a corridor that takes you to the other exhibition rooms. Let's go!" Together they edged their way around the crowd over to a door behind a large marble column. It was unlocked, and they crept out without being noticed. They passed through a narrow hallway with offices on one side. "The museum's administrative offices," Carlo explained. Then they took a left and entered a room bearing a sign that said *Galleria Etrusca*. "This is the exhibition room directly behind the main hall," Carlo informed her. Jada pulled the handle of the door between the *Galleria Etrusca* and the main hall to see if it would open from the other side, but it didn't budge. *It was clear that the tattooed man didn't want to be followed.* Jada scanned the dimly lit room, which was filled with glass cases housing vases and figurines and jewelry from Rome's Etruscan period, which predated the Roman Empire and lasted from around 800 BC to 500 BC.

Etruscan Vases

Six feet above them a mezzanine level displaying more artifacts ran along the perimeter of the room. A number of marble pillars stood behind the railing along the mezzanine, each topped with a large brown and black urn decorated with different depictions of hunters, horses, and other scenes of Etruscan life. Jada noticed something on the floor near a case that contained Etruscan jewelry. *Could it be a clue or just a tissue some tourist dropped?* she thought as she went over to have a look. As she got closer she saw that it was not a tissue, but a crumpled pale green latex glove. Carlo bent to pick it up.

"Don't!" she cried. "It may have fingerprints on it. We have to tell the police. This could belong to whoever stole the scepter. The thief probably used gloves to carry it and may have dropped one." Jada took out her cell phone and took a few pictures of the glove. "See any other clues?" she asked Carlo, looking around the room. Just then, from the corner of her eye, she saw a shadow moving above them, and they both heard a loud scraping sound. "Watch out!" Jada cried and pushed Carlo out of the way just as a huge ceramic vase fell from the level above and crashed to the floor right where they had been standing. They landed on the floor in a heap and covered in dust. Had Jada been a second slower, there would have been blood on the floor along with the fragments of a two-thousand-year-old ceramic. "Are you OK?" Jada asked Carlo.

"*Sì*. I mean, yes. You?" Carlo replied, wiping his eyes before looking at Jada with concern.

Jada coughed, wondering how dangerous it was to inhale two-thousand-year-old dust. "I'm OK. What just happened?" Frowning, Jada looked up. "That thing didn't just fall from the sky. How do we get up there?"

"This way!" Carlo responded. They leaped up, shook themselves off, and headed out the back door of the hall and up the stairs leading to the mezzanine. Jada tugged Carlo's sleeve and motioned for him to slow down. She put her finger to her lips to warn him to be quiet. Whoever had pushed the urn could still be there, and he seemed to have no problem trying to kill or at least maim them. They reached the top of the stairs.

"Light?" Jada whispered. Carlo pointed to a switch behind a case near the entryway. Jada had her cell phone ready and her camera function on. She wasn't going to try to stop a thief and attacker, but she could at least try to get proof of his identity for the police. She held up a finger. One. Then a second finger. Two. When she pointed three fingers at Carlo, he switched on the light. The mezzanine was illuminated . . . and they were alone. They walked among the display cases and examined the area around the empty pillar where the now shattered urn had stood, but there was no sign of anyone or any clues. They could see the entire exhibit hall below, and other than the debris on the floor from the urn and the crumpled glove, no one was there and nothing was amiss. "Are there other exits?" Jada asked.

"Just the back one," he replied. "It leads out onto a patio for visitors."

"Show me," she said. They walked through the two other halls on the main floor of the museum and stopped at the back exit. Jada examined the door, but found no signs of tampering. "Either the thief was let in by someone inside the museum or he entered through the front door, likely as a guest of tonight's reception," she surmised. They stepped outside. There was a food truck parked to the side of the patio. "It belongs to the caterers," Jada said, pointing to the sign on the side. She noticed a set of tire marks in front of and to the left of the truck. "Another vehicle was here," Jada said, bending down to examine the marks on the ground. "See, the marks are narrower than the tires of the truck. Let's find out if the caterers used a second vehicle. If not, the thief probably made his getaway from here," she said, snapping a photo of the tread marks.

Jada and Carlo returned to the reception hall to find it swarming with police. The guests had been divided into groups, and detectives were interviewing them. "No, Detective. I told you this door was locked the entire time," Carlo overheard the guard who had been stationed at the door to the *Galleria Etrusca* exclaim loudly in Italian to the detective who was questioning him. The detective was a tall, attractive woman in her mid-forties, with shoulder-length auburn hair and hazel eyes. She wore a dark pantsuit and sensible loafers, but in a nod to fashion, had on a designer belt with interlocking gold G's. The two teens approached the detective and the guard.

"Jada, tell the detective what you saw," Carlo said. He then spoke in Italian to the detective, "*Questa ragazza ha visto un uomo uscendo da questa porta durante il ricevimento.* This girl saw a man leaving through this door during the reception."

"Is this true?" the detective asked Jada in perfect but accented English.

"Yes," Jada replied. She proceeded to tell the detective everything she had seen and how they had been attacked with the urn. The guard tried to interrupt Jada, but the detective sharply told him to be quiet and to wait by the door. He slunk away and glared at Jada from his post. Jada showed the detective the latex glove and the shattered urn as well as the tire marks outside and shared her theories about the crime. "I think you definitely want to question the caterers to see if they brought a second car, which is doubtful in my view, because I believe the tire marks out back belong to the thief's getaway car."

"Very impressive, *signorina*," the detective complimented Jada. "You have given us some valuable leads. You two narrowly escaped danger. The thief or thieves will have to answer for the attempt to harm you and the destroyed urn, as well as for the missing scepter. I have no doubt the two incidents are related. Here is my card. My name is Commissario Ruffalo, and I'm in charge of this investigation. If you remember anything else, please give me a call. In the meantime," she said, leading Jada and Carlo back to the reception hall, "let's find your parents. I need your contact information while you are in Rome in case we need to reach you to question you further."

Jada wanted to stay to watch the police work but her parents insisted they return to the hotel once they had been okayed to leave by the police. With her parents' approval, she and Carlo exchanged phone numbers and agreed to get together to go sightseeing around Rome.

# CHAPTER 5

"What a night!" Jada's mom commented as the family had breakfast in their suite the next morning. They each wore a plush white terrycloth bathrobe with the insignia of the hotel on the front.

"Where's the bacon? What, no eggs?" Justin exclaimed as he sat down and surveyed the table.

"It's called continental breakfast, J. As in the continent of Europe, of which Italy is a country," Jada said, only a little snarkily. "Here they have a light breakfast. These croissants are delicious," she said, dunking the end of one into her hot chocolate.

"I don't know if I'd call this breakfast light," Mrs. Johnson said, eyeing the basket of croissants and pastries, pile of toast, assorted jams, butter, fruit plate, selection of yogurts, and juice, milk, coffee, and hot chocolate that laded the table.

"*Cornetto,*" Justin corrected Jada as he ate half of his in one bite. "That's Italian for croissant. See, I know more Italian than you do even though you've got an Italian boyfriend." Mr. Johnson looked up from his paper in mock alarm.

"I do not," Jada cried, but before they could engage in a full-blown argument, Mr. Johnson shushed them.

"Have I told you kids about the deal I'm working on with Augusto Boroni?" he asked.

Their dad always gave them a short explanation of the deals that kept him so busy, and Jada and Justin were actually interested in hearing about his work. Justin planned to be a businessman like his dad when

20

he grew up, and lately, Jada, who had always wanted to pursue some type of law enforcement career, had been thinking of specializing in fighting corporate espionage. She had seen a documentary about it on television. Lots of foreign companies spied on American ones to steal corporate know-how and designs, and law enforcement agents were needed to fight this type of crime.

"So you know," Mr. Johnson began, "that the company I work for is a conglomerate, which means we own many types of businesses. Industria Boroni is an Italian food company. They make pasta, sauces, olive oil, baked goods, you name it. Go into any Italian supermarket or any Italian kitchen and you will find boxes and bottles with the Boroni label on them. Problem is, they're now facing competition from new food companies and a changing marketplace. Also, from what I understand, things started going downhill for the company when Augusto Boroni's son, Giovanni, took over from him as chief executive officer. A CEO runs a company day to day. Giovanni made some bad decisions, and now what used to be a really solid company is in financial trouble."

"That's where you guys come in, right, Dad?"

"Exactly, Jada. We plan to buy the company and significantly increase the export of their products to the US and other countries around the world. Their factories will remain productive, and we may even need to hire more Italian workers. We also plan to start producing products in the US using their recipes, so we'll be creating jobs in America, as well as providing work for American farmers who will supply us. Often when two companies merge, some employees lose their jobs. But in this case, because Italian food production is a new business for us, we plan to do the opposite and hire more workers."

"Your deal sounds like a win/win situation," Justin said, trying to sound grown-up.

"It should be," replied Mr. Johnson. "Even deals that make good sense for both parties, like this one, take time and negotiation to complete. There's a long list of steps that have to be taken to buy a company. The buyer has to learn all about the target company—about its operations, financial position, assets, debts, legal liabilities. This investigation is called 'due diligence.' After that's completed, then the buyer has to value the company and agree with the seller on a price. This deal is being made even more complicated because Giovanni, the CEO, doesn't want to sell. He's doing everything he can to change his father's mind and to kill the deal."

"But why?" Jada asked.

"Pride, I suppose. The business has been in his family for generations, and it's his turn to run it. He views his position as head of the company as a birthright and not something he needs to earn by hard work, good judgment, and great business skills. He knows that once we buy it, we'll replace him with a new, more competent CEO. Anyway, the decision whether or not to do the deal is not his alone. Industria Boroni is a family business; all of the members of the Boroni family are the shareholders or owners. The shareholders will vote, and if the majority votes for the deal, then my company, AmeriFoods, gets to buy Industria Boroni. And with that said, I'd better get to it." Mr. Johnson stood up and went to get dressed for work.

Jada headed to the gym for a quick workout to beat jet lag. "*Signorina.* Signorina Johnson," the clerk at the front desk of the hotel called to Jada as she entered the lobby on her way to the fitness center. "I have an urgent message for you. I was about to send it up to your room. The courier requested that it be hand delivered to you personally."

Jada took the folded piece of paper from the clerk and opened it.

*St. Peter's Basilica is a church you should see*
*It's housed in the heart of Vatican City*
*Under the altar is St. Peter's grave*
*Bernini's Canopy in the center of the nave*
*This four-poster bronze sculpture is more than just art*
*It's where a planned meeting will have its start*
*I think what will be said, you will want to hear*
*Find the scarred, tattooed man and a man with a beard*

*Look, listen, but don't let them see you*
*Their rendezvous is tomorrow at two*

———*Un amica*

The clerk had no idea of the identity of the sender, but confirmed to Jada that "*amica*" meant "female friend." Someone had sent her an anonymous clue! Maybe it would lead to the thief of the scepter.

# CHAPTER 6

Bernini's Canopy

Jada did her best thinking when running. She reread the message from her *amica* a number of times while on the treadmill. *The scarred, tattooed man in the poem must be the guy from the plane who keeps eluding me,* Jada reasoned. *But who is the bearded man? Why are they meeting? And why on earth does someone calling herself my friend want me to know about it?*

Back in the suite, Jada got out her guidebook and read about St. Peter's Basilica, considered the holiest and most famous Catholic church; and the Vatican, the home of the head of the church, the pope. She convinced Justin to visit the Vatican with her while their mother did some shopping.

It was half past one when the taxi let them off at the entrance to St. Peter's Square. Throngs of tourists from all over the world, dressed in their country's version of American-style casual wear, milled around in the huge square or *piazza*. Jada checked her watch before heading toward the entrance. She hadn't told anyone about her secret mission, and was about to fill Justin in and instruct him to stay away from Bernini's Canopy to avoid being recognized by the tattooed man. But Justin had his own plans. "J, I'm going to head over to the Sistine Chapel," he said, pulling his sketchpad out of his backpack. "I want to try to copy 'the touch' where God gives life to Adam. Want to come with me?" The Sistine Chapel is located in the Vatican museum, adjacent to St. Peter's. Completed in 1512, its painted ceiling is one of Michelangelo's masterpieces, depicting biblical stories from the creation of the world to Judgment Day in glorious color and detail.

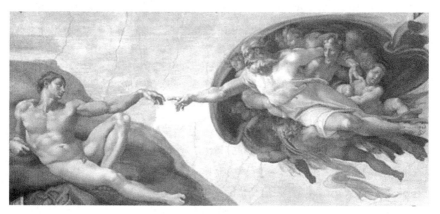

Sistine Chapel Ceiling

"You could have told me . . .," Jada started and then stopped herself. Ordinarily, she would have given her brother a hard time about his habit of changing plans without warning, but this time she was glad to be left on her own to conduct her detective work. So instead of scolding him, she readily agreed to meet him back at the hotel later.

With Justin gone, Jada reached into her straw shoulder bag and pulled out her disguise. There was a strict dress code to enter the church. Visitors were required to cover their shoulders and knees in respect, and many women carried a scarf or shawl that they could wrap around their shoulders or tie around their waists before entering if what they were wearing was inappropriate. Some of the most devoutly religious women covered their heads as well. Jada put an African batik scarf she'd borrowed from her mother over her head, then donned a pair of tinted glasses. She had deliberately worn flat sandals instead of sneakers, and had left her purple backpack behind as well. She hoped that at a glance she appeared to be a religious African woman rather an Black American teenage detective.

On the way into the basilica, Jada passed a number of colorfully dressed sentries guarding the building. She had read in her guidebook that the Swiss Guard, responsible for the security of the pope and the Vatican since the 1500s, wear the same uniform today that they have worn for the past almost five hundred years—a yellow, blue, and red striped jacket with knee britches of the same colors, yellow and blue stockings, a white ruffled collar, white gloves, red wristlets, black shoes, and a black beret. Jada snapped a picture of one of the guards before going inside the church.

Swiss Guards

Jada took up position in a niche inside the basilica opposite the enormous bronze canopy marking the tomb of St. Peter. She pretended to examine a sculpture, making sure to maintain an oblique view of the canopy. Hundreds of tourists milled around the cavernous church, taking in all the opulent artwork and decorations on the walls, ceiling, and floor. If *MTV Cribs* had existed in the 1500s, St. Peter's would've been on the premier episode. *God's house, decorated by the Catholic Church.* Jada smiled at the thought while scrutinizing the crowd for the subjects of her surveillance. There were a lot of bearded men dotted among the crowd of tourists. But after circling it a few times, one gray-bearded gentleman stopped next to one of the canopy's pillars clearly pretending to study his guidebook while surreptitiously surveying the room. He looked to be in his late sixties and was elegantly dressed, wearing a linen sports jacket and tasseled loafers despite the summer heat. He leaned on a polished wooden walking stick with a silver handle. A few minutes later Jada tensed up and felt her heart quicken as she spotted the tattooed man from the plane approaching the gray-bearded man with the cane. Today there was no mistaking the dark ink that stained his neck, an eagle in flight, visibly emerging from his T-shirt.

The two men began whispering to each other, which was not unusual since loud talking was forbidden in the church. Jada strained to hear what they were saying but couldn't pick up a word, and she wasn't able to read their lips since she couldn't stare directly at them for fear of attracting their attention. The bearded man motioned to his tattooed associate, and they turned and headed toward the pews at the front of the church. Jada noticed the bearded man walking with a slight limp; that must be why he was carrying a cane and wanted to sit. Jada quietly slipped into a pew two rows behind them, praying her disguise was good enough. There were quite a few tourists taking a rest from sightseeing, and a few older women praying, so Jada hoped she was not conspicuous. The two men spoke to each other in English with different accents.

"Object is ready for delivery, *Monsieur* Paul," the tattooed man said.

"Very good, Ivan," the bearded man responded. "Our buyer will be very pleased to hear it. You have disguised it properly?"

"Hidden inside a shipment of goods, as you instructed," Ivan said.

"Good. I will contact you when it is time for the handover, in about a week. You have something for me, do you not?" *Monsieur* Paul asked. Ivan handed him an envelope, which *Monsieur* Paul peered into before placing it inside his guidebook. "Very good. Everything the client needs to collect the item when it arrives in Russia—invoice and bill of sale for the shipment, plus completed customs papers."

"Yes, yes," Ivan replied.

"You can rely on my expertise and connections to get it from Italy into Russia," *Monsieur* Paul replied smoothly.

"OK. Now, you make phone call," Ivan said bluntly.

"Not here," *Monsieur* Paul responded. "Cell phone use is not permitted in the basilica. I'll do it as soon as I leave."

"No!" Ivan said, raising his voice above a whisper. He looked around to see if anyone had noticed, and Jada lowered her head as if in prayer to hide her face. "Buyer must wire funds, and I confirm receipt before we go. Five million today, fifty million on delivery in St. Petersburg. That was the deal!"

"The deal was also that this exchange would be quick so that we aren't seen together. Fine! I will go outside and make the call to wire the funds. You follow me in a few minutes. I'll wait near the obelisk so you can see me. When the call is done, you can check if the funds have hit your employer's account. When the payment has gone through, you walk past me and leave. I will stay at the obelisk until I see you go away. Does that work to your satisfaction?" *Monsieur* Paul asked.

Ivan grunted his assent. *They must be talking about the scepter and they are planning to smuggle it out of Italy. I've got to have proof of this meeting before they split up*, Jada thought. *Monsieur* Paul gathered his cane and his guidebook and was about to stand. He turned slightly to nod goodbye to Ivan. Jada grabbed her phone and opened the camera app. She pretended to take a picture of the altar in front of them, but instead took a photo of the two men facing each other in profile, forgetting to change the settings to remove the flash function. The two men turned to the source of the bright light, and at the same time a guard hastened over to Jada. "*Signorina*! Flash photography is not allowed in the basilica," he snapped, his voice carrying in the hushed church. All eyes were on Jada, and the tattooed man's eyes widened in recognition. She needed to get out of there fast.

"*Scusi*," Jada muttered, and grabbed her bag and hurried out of the pew, slipping into the tide of tourists strolling past. She moved quickly to put distance between herself and the two men, but didn't run. She knew she was safe inside the enormous basilica; after all, they couldn't very well attack her in the most famous place of worship in the world with hundreds of tourists as witnesses. But once she was outside she was fair game. Jada bided her time, pretending to view the artwork, moving with the flow of the crowd, holding firmly to her bag containing the iPhone with the picture on it, and checking behind her to keep track of the two men. They had split up. *Monsieur* Paul limped purposefully to the front entrance of St. Peter's and exited without looking back. Perhaps he was setting a trap and would be waiting for her when she got outside. But Jada didn't think so. She couldn't be sure, but Jada bet he had gone to avoid involvement and had left Ivan to deal with her.

Jada approached the famous sculpture, *La Pieta*, the first major work of art near the entrance to St. Peter's. She was almost at the door. Despite her sense of alarm, Jada couldn't help being moved by the beauty of Michelangelo's marble statue of Mary holding the body of Jesus after the crucifixion. It was displayed behind bulletproof glass because in the 1970s a deranged man had attacked the statue with a hammer,

knocking off Mary's arm and damaging her face. The statue had been restored to perfection by master artists, but the added protection of bulletproof glass reminded Jada that security at the entrance of St. Peter's was not foolproof. She knew that Ivan could very well be armed, and it was clear that he was a dangerous man.

Jada maneuvered herself into the very center of the

The Pieta

crowd in front of the *Pieta*, among tourists who had just entered the church. She turned to see Ivan about ten feet behind her at the edge of the crowd. Jada had an idea. She took out her phone again, made sure the flash was on and started taking pictures of the famous statue. Not realizing flash photography was forbidden, many other tourists followed suit, and soon there was a lightning storm of flashes compounded by their reflection by the bulletproof glass. A swarm of guards rushed over in alarm at the mass breach of the rules. *"Arrete!" "Fermez!" "Para!" "Halt an*!" "*Tingzhi*!" "*Basta*!" "STOP!" in multiple languages rang through the air as the guards attempted to enforce the flash ban, even daring to try to confiscate the cameras of some. A large red-faced man did not take kindly to a guard half his size pulling at the camera around his neck and unleashed a tirade in German that was likely not appropriate language for inside a church. An elderly Indian woman in a sari raised her selfie stick menacingly at the guard who had threatened to take her phone. A group of teenage boys in England soccer jerseys grabbed the hat of one of the guards and started playing keep away with it. In the mayhem that had escalated into an international incident, Jada slipped through the crowd and strode quickly out the door.

Outside, at the corner of the building, were stationed two Swiss guardsmen who were oblivious to the scene playing out inside. In their colorful uniforms, they were easy to spot even in a haze of adrenaline. "Excuse me, sir. Do you speak English?" Jada asked one of the guards as the other posed for a photo with two teenage tourists. The girls giggled as they took turns taking pictures with the tall handsome young man in his funny outfit.

"Yes, how can I help you?" the guard replied, probably expecting another request for a photo rather than an actual security issue.

"There is a man in the basilica who is acting kind of crazy. He's saying some awful things about the pope, and he says he's going to burn St. Peter's down. He's really big, and he's got this weird tattoo on his neck that looks like some sort of satanic symbol." Jada took off her glasses, and her eyes were wide with fear and welling with tears. Just then, Ivan stormed out of the door to the church, looking around wildly for Jada. "There he is," Jada cried, pointing.

"*Codice Rosso*! Code Red!" the guard shouted to his fellow guardsmen, and they ran at Ivan, the two teenage girls filming them in action on their phones. It took Ivan a moment to register that he was the target of their chase, and he looked like a deer in headlights deciding whether to stand firm or flee. Flight won out, and Ivan took off, sprinting across the *piazza* with the two brightly colored guards on his tail. Jada wanted to avoid interrogation by the Swiss Guard or attack by Ivan should he elude the guardsmen. She spotted a large group of what appeared to be

Black American tourists walking together in the middle of the *piazza*. She decided to hide in plain site by joining the group. She slipped the batik scarf off her head and into her bag, put her sunglasses on again, and sidled up to the group as they listened to their tour guide.

"Aren't you Delia's niece?" one of the elderly ladies on the tour asked her. Jada smiled at her and pretended to be engrossed in the history lesson being given by the tour guide. "Delia's niece sure has grown," the lady said to her friend next to her.

"Pretty as a picture," the other old lady added. "Reminds me of my granddaughter." Jada walked on the edge of the tourist group, frequently checking around her for the tattooed Ivan by pretending to take pictures of St. Peter's church and square. Finally, they arrived at the group's tour bus, which was parked outside the *piazza* next to a taxi stand.

"Enjoy Rome!" Jada called to the two ladies who had chatted to her, as she hopped in a cab, relieved to have avoided danger. She waved at the perplexed grandmothers as the taxi sped away.

# CHAPTER 7

Rome Colosseum

Fueled by adrenaline and jet lag, Jada stayed up with Justin until the wee hours of the morning analyzing what she had seen and heard at the Vatican. After too few hours of sleep, the siblings took an Uber to meet Carlo at the Roman Colosseum, a huge ancient stone-and-concrete structure, breathtaking in size and beauty. Standing in front of it, they felt transported to ancient times. Its curved wall is broken off in part, and the portion of the wall still standing is lined with arched window openings. Jada's guidebook said that the windows used to house statues of Roman gods and other figures from mythology.

"*Ciao!*" Carlo called out when he saw them.

"*Ciao!*" Jada and Justin responded in unison. As they waited in line to enter, Jada checked her phone repeatedly. Jada had texted Commissario Ruffalo immediately after her Vatican adventure, and was still waiting for a response. She filled Carlo in on the conversation between the scarred, tattooed man—who now had a name, Ivan—and the mysterious *Monsieur* Paul.

"Jada, the police need to know about this. Things can move a little slower in Italy in the summertime. If you don't hear from the *commissario* by tomorrow, I'll go with you to police headquarters to make a report," Carlo offered.

"Good plan. Thanks," Jada replied, grateful to have her new Italian-speaking friend help her on the case.

They entered the Colosseum after passing through metal detectors like at an airport. "Roman history is my hobby," Carlo told Jada and Justin, "so I'm happy to be your tour guide. The Colosseum was a huge ancient Roman amphitheater, built in AD 70–80. It was the ancient equivalent of a sports stadium that could hold between 50,000 and 80,000 spectators."

"Modern American football stadiums usually hold about that many people," Justin informed them.

"Same for European soccer stadiums," Carlo added. "But the ancient Romans didn't come to the Colosseum to watch American football or soccer."

"They came to watch gladiators," Jada offered.

"*Esatto.* Exactly," Carlo said as they strolled along the perimeter of the interior of the Colosseum, looking down on the tiers of stone that would have been seats for spectators and the floor of the arena where the action took place. "Often the gladiators fought to the death. When a gladiator was clearly about to lose, he would bend on one knee and raise his left hand. The other gladiator remained poised with his sword to finish him off. Then the crowd got to decide the fate of the defeated warrior. If they thought he had fought valiantly, they would give a hand gesture, the thumbs-down signal, to say let him live. If they thought he had fought badly and deserved to die, they would give thumbs-up, signaling they wanted the defeated gladiator to be killed. A judge would assess the crowd and give his verdict based on what the majority wanted."

"Wait, so thumbs-up meant 'kill him'? We use thumbs-up as a sign of approval," Justin said.

"They did too," Jada answered. "Approval to kill."

# CHAPTER 8

Circus Maximus

The trio headed out of the Colosseum and walked down Via di San Gregorio, a major thoroughfare. Cars zoomed by, drivers ignoring the faded dotted lines delineating lanes. Motor scooters weaved in and out of traffic. Horns beeped, and there was the occasional shout of a driver protesting being cut off by another car. A tourist tried to cross the road at a pedestrian crosswalk, but he waited in vain since no one stopped or even slowed down to let him pass. Finally, there was a break in the traffic, and he was able to dart quickly across the street.

"This way to the Circus Maximus where the ancient Romans had chariot races," Carlo said, in the lead. "It's a public park now, a long grassy field overlaying the ruins of the original ancient racetrack deep underground, but you can still imagine horses and chariots racing down the course."

"Carlo," Jada began, about to ask about the driving age in Italy, when she felt a strong tug that sent her tumbling to the ground. "My backpack!" she cried, as a small girl in tattered, mismatched clothing sprinted down the street, Jada's purple backpack slung over her shoulder. Jada's jeans were ripped at the knee and her hand was badly scraped where she used it to break her fall.

"Are you OK?" Justin asked as he and Carlo bent down to examine her blood-streaked hand and then helped her to her feet.

"Thanks, I'm fine. She's getting away. Let's go!" Jada shouted and started running in the direction the girl had gone. Carlo and Justin took off behind Jada. Each of the boys took a different side street in case the girl had turned left or right. Jada's intuition told her to keep straight, and soon enough, she spied her purple backpack on the back of the fleet-footed, dark-haired girl up ahead. Jada spotted a vast open expanse of green to the right. *That must be the Circus Maximus,* she thought.

Luckily, the traffic of Rome was on Jada's side. Rush hour was approaching, and the Via di San Gregorio was a rushing river of cars. To cross it at a pedestrian crosswalk would be to risk death, and there wasn't a stoplight in sight. The girl had no choice but to turn right and run through the Circus Maximus, where Jada had a chance to overtake her. The girl had a considerable lead, but Jada was a sprinter on her school's track team. And while Jada's white sneakers might have identified her as an American tourist, they were better for running than the girl's worn sandals.

"Stop! Stop!" Jada yelled, hoping the girl would know what the word meant. If she did, she didn't show it. At about a third of the length of the field, Jada caught up to her, reached out, grabbed the handle at the top of her backpack, and yanked hard. The girl tumbled backward and hit the ground with a thud, landing on her right shoulder. Before she could recover, Jada pulled the backpack off and tossed it to one side. The girl scrambled to get up, holding her right shoulder with her left hand as if in serious pain. Her right arm hung limply at her side. Jada felt sorry she had knocked her to the ground so forcefully. "Are you OK?" Jada asked with concern, hoping the girl would understand from her tone, if not her words, that she hadn't meant to hurt her. The girl mumbled something unintelligible and then all of a sudden took off, both arms pumping furiously. *That little faker!* Jada thought, and quickly strapped on her backpack and took off after the girl a second time. This time she had reinforcements. To Jada's relief, she saw Justin and Carlo running toward them from either side of the park. The girl was trapped. She dropped to one knee, panting hard, and Jada was reminded of the sign of surrender of the gladiators.

"*Lladra!* Thief!" Carlo shouted at the girl in Italian. He then proceeded to chastise her, and judging from the number of times the word "*carabinieri*" was used, threatened to turn her over to the police. Jada and Justin didn't understand what the girl said in return, but they assumed she was begging them not to involve the police. At a certain point, Carlo's eyes widened in surprise.

"What did she say?" Jada asked.

"I had assumed she was just a petty thief," Carlo replied. "But she says a man paid her to steal your backpack."

"What? Who?" Jada asked in surprise. She turned to the girl. "What did he look like?" Carlo translated her question and the girl's response.

"She says he had a large tattoo of a winged bird on his neck and a long scar on his face. He gave her twenty euros to steal the backpack, and he told her she could keep the backpack and its contents once she had stolen it."

"Ivan," Jada cried. Her mind was racing. She had to find out who Ivan was and why he was harassing her.

"We ought to get the police," Justin said. The girl clearly understood some English because at the word "police" she started to cry.

Jada asked the girl, who told them her name was Rosela, a few more questions with Carlo acting as interpreter, and got some additional information. The man had approached Rosela as she was begging for money from tourists near the Colosseum. He had pointed Jada out to her as Jada was entering the Colosseum. He didn't speak Italian very well, but he had managed to tell her that Jada was a rude American with whom he had argued, and he wanted to get back at her. He had also said there was a lot of cash in the backpack that Rosela would get to keep.

Jada felt sorry for the girl. Close up she realized that even though Rosela was much smaller, she was about Jada's own age. "Tell her we won't report her to the police," Jada said to Carlo. "Can I give Rosela your cell number since I doubt she has the money to make an international call to my US number?" Jada took a pen and small notepad out of her backpack and handed it to Carlo who scribbled down his number. Jada addressed Rosela directly. "That man is dangerous. If he contacts you again or if you see him around, please give us a call." Carlo translated for Rosela, handing her the slip of paper. Rosela shoved it in her pocket and ran off without a word.

# CHAPTER 9

The next day Jada and her family were invited to accompany her father on a tour of the Boroni manufacturing plant, a gleaming modern white and steel-gray facility that seemed more like a nuclear plant than a place that made food. Their guide was Anna Conti, senior manager of the plant. Dressed like factory employees in white coats and white hats that looked like shower caps, the Jones family toured the part of the plant where pasta was made. The whir of machines filled the air, and Anna Conti had to shout to be heard over the din.

"The first step in the pasta production process," she said, "is the mixing of the dough. After the mixer, the dough is either molded or rolled. Both molded pasta and rolled pasta need to be cut and dried," Anna Conti continued as they moved along the production line. The blade of a large cutting machine moved almost faster than Jada's eyes could register, and cut pasta twists fell into a vat underneath.

Something else caught her eye. Jada and her family had been outfitted in Boroni factory worker clothes, but there was something the employees wore that she and her family did not—light green latex gloves. The gloves the Boroni workers were wearing were the exact color of the crumpled glove she had found on the floor of the museum the night the scepter went missing. Jada wondered if latex gloves in this particular color were commonplace in Italy. In the US, latex gloves were usually white.

Anna Conti asked, "Are there any questions about the Boroni pasta production process?"

Jada immediately raised her hand. Her mother smiled at her daughter's curiosity. "Are factory workers wearing latex gloves for hygiene purposes?" Jada asked.

"Yes, absolutely," Anna Conti replied. "All factory employees who work in the area where the pasta is produced must wear gloves to keep the product clean and free from impurities."

"And are these green latex gloves common in Italy or do only Boroni employees wear this type of glove?" Jada followed up. Her mother frowned quizzically at Jada's questions about gloves rather than pasta.

"The gloves worn by our workers are produced especially for Industria Boroni by a factory outside of Milan. We special order our gloves in the same shade of Boroni green that is on our packaging," Anna Conti answered. She turned to continue along the production line.

"Would it be possible," Jada piped up again, "to have a pair of these gloves? Umm . . . as a souvenir of our visit." Mr. Johnson gave his daughter a look that said "you're pushing it," and Jada knew she would have to explain to her parents later why she was so interested in the gloves.

"Well, we usually give our visitors a gift basket of pastas and sauces and other Boroni products at the end of the tour, but I'm sure we can find a pair of gloves for the *signorina* as well, if this is what she would like," Anna Conti responded, seeming puzzled by Jada's odd request. "And now we come to my favorite part of the tour," she continued. "Lunch!"

Jada and Justin headed straight to the pizza bar in the factory dining room. The thin-crust pizza was rectangular in shape, and came with every topping imaginable. There was sausage pizza, mushroom pizza, anchovy pizza, and of course pizza *margherita* with tomato, mozzarella, and basil. But there was also pizza *rossa*, which is pizza with just tomato sauce and no cheese, as well as pizza with toppings they had never heard of, such as pumpkin flower and radicchio. There was even a white pizza with no tomato sauce, topped with sliced potatoes and sprinkled with rosemary. They pointed to the type they wanted. The server indicated where he was about to cut, and they responded by gesturing to say if the piece was too big, too small, or just right. He then used scissors to cut the pizza into a rectangular slice.

"I thought pizza was supposed to be round," Justin exclaimed as they sat down at a table with Mrs. Johnson and Anna Conti.

"Pizza *a taglio*, or the cut pizza you have here, is rectangular and is prepared in advance, and then heated up when served. In Italy it is usually sold in small shops throughout the day and evening, and you usually eat standing up at the counter. If you go to a restaurant in Italy, they will serve pizza only for dinner, and it will be round and made to order," Anna Conti explained.

As Anna spoke, Jada saw her father stop to chat with a man who was sitting at a corner table by himself at the end of the dining room. The Italian man looked to be in his early forties and was dressed impeccably in a dark suit and white shirt, open at the collar. He wore no tie, and a hint of gold sparkled from a chain around his neck. His wavy jet-black hair was perfectly coifed, with not a strand out of place. Jada noticed a gold pinkie ring on his hand that glinted in the light when he gestured. He was handsome, but Jada could read the arrogance on his face even from across the room. Jada couldn't hear the conversation, but her dad's demeanor was businesslike and polite. She could tell that the Italian man's responses were curt, and at times he gazed disinterestedly out of the window as her father spoke. After a few moments, Mr. Johnson nodded goodbye and joined his family and Anna Conti at their table.

"Who was that?" Mrs. Johnson asked, having witnessed the conversation as well.

"Giovanni Boroni, son of Augusto, father of Carlo, and CEO of Industria Boroni," Mr. Johnson replied.

"He didn't seem happy to talk to you," Justin blurted out.

Anna Conti shifted uncomfortably in her chair. Giovanni Boroni was her boss. She leaned forward and whispered conspiratorially, "He isn't happy to talk with anyone. Industria Boroni is a family business, and we employees get to know more about the family than we probably should. I hear Giovanni has always been an unpleasant person, but since his wife died he has become more and more hateful. It cannot be easy having Giovanni for a father. Carlo is fortunate his grandfather is such an important part of his life."

Just then shouting erupted at the corner table. Giovanni was berating a man for being five minutes late for lunch. He then started criticizing his work, tearing apart a report the poor guy had written, and finally blaming him for a delay in the rollout of a new product line. Everyone in the room tried to pretend they were having lunch as usual, but all had one eye and one ear on the loud scene playing out at the corner table. Anna Conti pretended to converse genially with the Johnson family, but she was really translating what was being shouted by Giovanni for them.

His final word needed no translation. "*Imbecile!*" Giovanni spat out before standing up and throwing his bread roll to the table. It landed in the manager's bowl, splattering tomato soup all over him. Giovanni left the manager, whose face had turned as red as the soup that stained his shirt and tie, sitting alone in a stunned silence.

"I've had meetings with that man," Mr. Johnson told them. "His name is Enrico Mattoni. He's in charge of research and development. He's a good manager and someone we plan to keep on the management team after we buy the company." Mr. Johnson left unsaid that those were definitely *not* his company's plans for Giovanni.

"Enrico is Giovanni's younger cousin," Anna Conti whispered to them, "but as you saw, they aren't close. They say that Giovanni bullied Enrico when they were children. Later, Enrico tried to distance himself from Giovanni and escape the family business. He studied archeology instead of business as was expected of him, though for some reason he never got his degree. He ended up working here at Industria Boroni and until recently was doing well. As you said, Mr. Johnson, he is actually very good at his job. But now that Augusto has stepped down and Giovanni runs the company, Enrico finds himself in the very situation he always wanted to avoid, working for his cousin. Giovanni takes all the credit for Enrico's work and heaps as much criticism on him as possible. It is very unfair," she said, shaking her head. Jada could see her dad taking mental notes of everything Anna Conti had recounted.

Back at the hotel suite after lunch, Jada placed the Boroni gift basket they had gotten from the factory on the coffee table. She explained to her parents and Justin the reason behind her great interest in the Boroni factory gloves. She pulled a green latex glove from the gift basket and then pulled up the photo of the latex glove found at the museum on her phone. "Looks like an exact match," she exclaimed. Her family agreed. Jada found Commissario Ruffalo's business card and sent her another text.

# CHAPTER 10

Late that afternoon, Commissario Ruffalo met Jada at the front desk of the police station. "Detective Johnson!" she said to Jada with a wink, offering her hand. Jada shook it with a firm grip. "Thanks for your texts, and sorry I couldn't meet yesterday. I was in court testifying on another case. I believe you have something for me." Jada pulled the green gloves out of her backpack and handed them over.

She then told the *commissario* in greater detail about her stolen backpack instigated by Ivan, the message from an *amica*, and what had happened at the Vatican. Jada Airdropped the photo of Ivan and *Monsieur* Paul onto the *commissario*'s phone. "Jada, this is most interesting information," the *Commissario* said. "We'll see right away if we can use these pictures to identify Ivan and *Monsieur* Paul from our databases."

A young officer joined them. "Donetti, this is Signorina Johnson. She's been helping us with the museum case. Take these gloves to the lab and then meet us in Room 4," the *commissario* ordered. Donetti hurried off.

"We were only able to get a partial fingerprint on the glove from the crime scene," the *Commissario* said, turning back to Jada, "and so far, no matches with our database of criminals in Italy. I'm still waiting for a response from Interpol, the International Police Organization. You have given us a number of leads, so I think it is only fair to update you on what the investigation has turned up based on your help. The tire marks were indeed from a second car parked in back of the museum on the night of the theft, and this car did not belong to the caterers. They were marks from the tires of a Fiat Cinquecento (500), which unfortunately is quite a popular car here in Italy. But it is something of a coincidence that Marco Vitti, the assistant director of the museum, owns a 500. We're expecting Vitti here at any moment for an interview. Would you like to observe?"

Jada couldn't believe her luck. She followed the *commissario* to a room with a table, two chairs, and a glass window the length of one wall. The window looked onto an interrogation room similar to the one they were in. Donetti joined them. "When this switch is on," the *commissario* said, pointing to a black switch on the table in front of them, "you will be able to hear the other interrogation room. Donetti will fill you in on what is said."

Commissario Ruffalo led Marco Vitti into the other interrogation room. With Donetti translating, Jada listened in. The conversation started off as a friendly chat. It was clear that Vitti enjoyed talking with an attractive woman, regardless of the circumstances. He cracked a few jokes, at which the *commissario* dutifully laughed, and then casually and conversationally, she started to ask questions. "So, Signor Vitti, tell me a bit about yourself. Where did you study and what did you do before coming to work at the Rome Museum of Art and Antiquities?"

"Well, I got my PhD in archeology at the University of Rome, and graduated at the top of my class," Vitti boasted. "Of course, with an academic record such as mine, it was only natural that I become a professor. I enjoyed teaching students and writing books on archeology, but when the university made a colleague head of the Department of Archeology instead of me, I decided to take my talents elsewhere."

"So you left the university when the assistant director job at the museum became available? Was that two years ago?" Commissario Ruffalo asked.

"I joined the museum two years ago, yes. I originally applied for the director position as was fitting for someone of my intellect and experience, but the museum trustees stupidly decided to give the director job to Teresa Fabbri and hired me as assistant director." Even without Donetti translating, Jada would have been able to tell from the tone of Vitti's voice and the sneer on his face when he said Fabbri's name that he was not fond of his boss.

"I bet they realize their error now that the scepter has been stolen. I would have focused more on security and less on party planning had I been the director," Vitti said. If the *commissario* was annoyed at the implicit sexism in Vitti's comment, she didn't show it, and instead nodded sympathetically. Encouraged, Vitti continued. "I should have been the one in charge of the exhibit since the archeological dig that unearthed the scepter was my project."

"So you discovered the ancient scepter?" the *commissario* asked, sounding impressed.

"Yes!" Vitti almost shouted. The *commissario* was so friendly and such a good listener that Vitti spoke freely. "It was my research that identified the area where the scepter was buried and my project to organize the dig. The discovery of the ancient scepter was mine, and Fabbri took all the credit."

"Very interesting. Now, let's discuss the night in question. Were you at the museum all day until the reception?" The air in the room changed as the *commissario* started asking specific questions about the night of the theft. Vitti answered warily as he finally remembered that this was not just a chat, but a formal interview with a police detective about a crime.

"No, I went home at about 4:30 to eat and change clothes."

"What time did you return to the museum?"

"Around 6:45."

"Was anyone with you between 4:30 and 6:45?"

"My wife came home from work to pick me up at around 6:30, and we went to the museum together."

"Did you take the Fiat 500?"

Vitti looked surprised that the *commissario* knew what kind of car he drove. He answered all the questions asked, but his guard was up, and he was no longer chatty.

"No, we took my wife's car. Should I contact my lawyer?" he asked abruptly.

The *commissario* laughed genially. "Not necessary. We are merely gathering information on everyone who was at the museum reception the night of the theft," she reassured him.

She made a few more friendly comments before escorting Vitti to the door, patting his back kindly and sending him on his way. It was a virtuoso performance. Commissario Ruffalo had managed to play "good cop" and "bad cop" all by herself.

"Your thoughts, Detective?" Commissario Ruffalo asked as she rejoined Jada and Donetti.

"Well," Jada began, "I always start with an analysis of MMO."

"MMO?" the *commissario* asked.

"Motive, means, and opportunity," Jada replied. "Working at the museum, Vitti definitely had the means and opportunity to steal the scepter. He was one of the few people who had full access to it. And he has no one to corroborate his explanation of how he spent his time for the two hours before the reception. Until today, we had no idea he had a motive. Now we know—he hates his boss. He thinks she has taken credit for the scepter's discovery and exhibition, and that his hard work has been stolen. What better way to discredit her than to steal the discovered artifact? Even if he has only 'borrowed' the scepter and finds a way to give it back to the museum without being found out as the thief, he has damaged her reputation as a museum director because a major historical artifact disappeared while she was in charge."

"I like your analysis," the *commissario* said. "So that's it? Case closed? We arrest Vitti?"

"Not yet," Jada responded. "This is just a theory. We keep an eye on him while pursuing other leads."

"Exactly. In the meantime, Jada, I will alert security at your hotel so that they will be on the lookout if Ivan attempts to bother you there. He could be dangerous, so if you see him, don't approach him on your own. Call me, and the police will handle it. You have been most helpful as usual, Detective," the *commissario* said with a smile. "Donetti, please drive Signorina Johnson back to her hotel."

# CHAPTER 11

The next day, Carlo invited Jada and Justin to spend the day with him and his grandparents on their boat. Jada changed outfits three times before settling on the classic outfit she had first put on over her bathing suit—denim shorts, a striped boat-neck T-shirt, and espadrilles. *Clichéd maybe, but cute and comfy*, she thought. She was excited to see Carlo again and go for a ride on the Mediterranean Sea. She was even more excited when she saw the Boronis' boat. *La Grande Fuga*, the Great Escape, was a two-hundred-foot yacht of gleaming white aluminum, polished teak wood, and shining silvery chrome. It was a huge floating apartment with a living room, dining room, kitchen, four bedrooms and five bathrooms, and multiple decks for sunning and relaxation. They sailed for about an hour under a scorching yellow sun that glistened off the turquoise blue waters of the Med before dropping anchor off the coast of Ponza, a small resort island seventy miles from Rome.

"Why don't you kids go off and explore," Augusto Boroni said to Jada, Justin, and Carlo. "There are a number of smaller uninhabited islands located around Ponza."

"Have fun, but be back at one for lunch," Gemma Boroni added. Jada was a good swimmer, but she didn't know if she could make it from the boat to shore under her own steam. Carlo saw the expression of concern on her face and motioned for her to look over the rail of the upper deck to the deck below. Three blue and white jet skis sat in a row. The crew hoisted the jet skis one at a time onto a mechanical lift that lowered them into the water, and after a brief tutorial on how to use them, the three teenagers were off. Jada felt incredibly *free* gliding along the water, salty spray on her skin, sun on her face, and wind in her hair.

Carlo, who had summered in Ponza every year of his life and knew the coastline and the islands like the back of his hand, led the way, followed by Jada, then Justin. Craggy rock formations formed natural arches that they drove under. *Grottos* or caves dotted the coastline, and Carlo led them toward one of the bigger ones and slowed down.

"Stay to your right as you enter the mouth of the cave," Carlo instructed. "There is a rock just below the surface in front of the cave that we have to avoid."

They followed him, slowly approaching the cave from the right, and immediately killed the engines of their jet skis once they were inside. It was dim in the grotto, and their voices echoed as the sound bounced off the cave walls. At first the amplified sound of the waves and the shadows on the walls of the cave were a little eerie, but once they got into the warm water and started to swim, Jada's trepidation washed away. The water was brilliantly blue-green and seemed to glow; Jada felt like she was inside a jewel. Swimming around, Jada noticed that it was brighter under the water than floating on top. Carlo explained that a hole in the cave wall below the surface of the water allowed sunlight in, which caused the water to be lit from below.

"I have another special place to show you," Carlo said as they climbed back onto their jet skis after their swim. Jada was glad for the relative darkness of the cave because she knew her ascent onto the jet ski from the water was not as dainty as when she had gotten on from the boat with a crew member's assistance. After slipping back into the water a few times, she finally made it on, and they inched out of the cave and then sped along the blue sea to a tiny island about 200 feet wide. They pulled their jet skis onto a beach made not of sand but of tiny smooth sand-colored pebbles that massaged the bottoms of their feet as they walked on them. They sat on the beach to hang out and chat. Jada lay down to sun herself. The pebbles beneath her were warm from the sun, causing heat to radiate from underneath her prone body while the sun toasted her from above. Jada sighed blissfully as she imagined steam rising from her wet skin and bathing suit as they dried.

"What is *that*?" Justin cried, rousing Jada from her state of Zen. Jada and Carlo sat up to see a massive slate gray behemoth of a boat approaching their little island. The prow was an arrow pointing directly at them, and they were clearly the target. The monster boat made the Boroni yacht look like a toy ship in a bathtub in comparison.

"They can't get near us in that thing," Jada declared. "I mean, the water's too shallow here, right?"

"It would get stuck on the rocks, true," Carlo responded. "But look," he said, pointing. Two men in black polo shirts and Bermuda shorts were hoisting a speedboat onto a mechanical lift similar to the one they had used for the jet skis. They were about to have company.

"I don't like the looks of this," Jada said. "Let's get out of here!" The three jumped up and dragged their jet skis into the water. Jada and Carlo gunned their engines, but Justin's jet ski wouldn't start. Jada and Carlo circled as he tried repeatedly to get the engine to turn over. The speedboat had been lowered into the water, and the two men were climbing aboard. Judging from the size of the outboard motor, it wouldn't take them long to reach the three teens. Jada hoped the feeling in her gut was wrong and that the two men would head in the opposite direction for an afternoon of fishing or snorkeling, but her fears were realized as she watched the speed boat take off, headed directly for them.

"Remove the fuel cap and see if you're out of gas," Carlo shouted suggestions to Justin to try to figure out what was wrong with the jet ski. Realizing they were running out of time, Jada decided to act.

"Get to the *Fuga*!" Jada cried. "I'm going to divert them!" Ignoring Justin's shouts not to leave by herself, Jada sped off to the west of the island along the route they had taken to get to the island from the cave. And sure enough, the speed boat changed course from heading to the island to following her. Jada's jet ski was fast, but it was no match for the powerful motorboat. She had to use its smaller size to her advantage. She steered in the direction of one of the larger islands they had passed that was surrounded by craggy rock formations. Jada and her jet ski weaved in and out of the rocky arches and between boulders rising out of the water. It was dangerous, she knew, and required deft handling of the jet ski, but it was effective at keeping the motorboat at bay. It was too large to maneuver the rocky path Jada was taking and had to stay farther seaward from the coastline than Jada. Still it followed her along a parallel trail.

Jada's mind raced as quickly as the jet ski. She spotted the grotto she and the boys had swum in earlier fifty yards away. She would have to race across open water to get to the entrance of the cave. Could she make it without the speedboat overtaking her? She decided she had to try. Abruptly she changed course and headed north, aiming directly at the center of the mouth of the cave. The speedboat followed her, right on her tail, so close that when she looked back she stared right into the steel blue eyes of the driver, whose gaze bored menacingly into her own. The other guy said something to the driver, and the speedboat slowed down a bit, the driver clearly assessing if he could fit into the entrance to the cave. He must have decided he could because Jada heard the speedboat's engine gun as he sped up directly behind her again.

Just as the jet ski approached the entrance to the cave, Jada veered sharply to the right, spraying water in her wake. The jet ski wobbled precariously, but Jada was able to keep control. The speedboat was not as agile as the jet ski, and was about to arc right in pursuit when *BAM!* It ran right into the rock beneath the water in front of the cave. There was a horrible screech of metal crashing into stone. The boat catapulted into the air and landed with a massive thud, sending a geyser of water spewing skyward. Its motor detached and lay sideways in the water, and the boat itself scraped against the rocks, non-navigable. Jada sped off to the *Fuga*, leaving the black-clad men in the water cursing and fuming.

Jada was pleased to find that Justin and Carlo had arrived at the *Fuga* just ahead of her. They had tethered Justin's jet ski to Carlo's, and they rode back together with the disabled jet ski trailing behind. "Jada!" they both called as she pulled up next to the yacht. They helped her aboard and the crew worked to hoist up her jet ski. She recounted what had happened to the boys and to Augusto and Gemma Boroni.

"Jada, that was brilliant!" Carlo said excitedly. "*Nonno*, let's go after the men. They may still be stranded on the rocks."

"Not so fast, Carlo. We don't know if they are armed. We'd better let the authorities handle this," Augusto Boroni replied.

"I'm calling the Coast Guard." Gemma Boroni rushed to get her cell phone.

Jada called Commissario Ruffalo to report what had happened. "Very dangerous, indeed," Commissario Ruffalo commented once she had heard Jada's story. "I'll call my colleagues at the Coast Guard as well to see if I can get a boat over there. It may be difficult. A cruise ship is in distress off the coast of Naples, so I believe most of their units have been deployed there. In the meantime, I have some information for you. The picture you sent me turned up one positive ID. Your tattooed man is a Bulgarian mobster named Ivan Golakov. He's wanted by Interpol in connection with an art theft in Belgium and another in the Netherlands. He's done time for all sorts of petty crimes and was once convicted of a brutal beating in London." Jada shuddered at the mention of the beating. She now knew what she'd suspected all along—Ivan was a violent criminal. The *commissario* continued, "I have a warrant out for his arrest as a 'person of interest.' Well done getting the picture to us. It was invaluable in identifying him."

"And the other man, *Monsieur* Paul?" Jada asked.

"Ah, that search was less conclusive," the *commissario* responded. "We were able to ID Ivan because he has a police record. His file includes mug shots of both full face and profile. *Monsieur* Paul must not have a police record, as his profile does not match any in our files. If I had a full frontal of his face, I could do a search using facial recognition software of government databases, driver's licenses, passports, and so on. But a profile shot does not help me with this. So he remains a mystery man."

"For now," Jada added.

# CHAPTER 12

*Ping!* Jada and Justin were strolling down Via dei Condotti, Rome's most exclusive shopping street, peering in the windows of Gucci, Prada, Bulgari and the flagship stores of the other major Italian fashion design houses, when Jada got a text message. She dug into her pocket for her phone, expecting the message to be from Carlo, whom they were on their way to meet. Instead it was from a blocked number and contained a startling message:

> *The drop was made, the pick up is soon*
> *You'll beat the receiver there if you get there by noon*
> *To transport the stolen relic, plans have been made*
> *Passage on a cargo train has been paid*
> *The documents are hidden where Christian bodies once lay*
> *Santa Priscilla protects them, and may she guide your way*
> *An urn in the Greek Chapel hides what you seek*
> *Put them back where you found them once you've had a peek*
> > *——Un amica*

Jada couldn't believe it. Another message from her "friend." She read the text aloud to Justin.

"Your friend's English is perfect," Justin commented. "And she seems to have a real knowledge of Rome."

"You are right," Jada responded, making a mental note of these traits of her *amica* that she would jot down in her notebook later as clues to her identity. "The 'stolen relic' she refers to must be the scepter," Jada added, as they now rushed to the Spanish Steps. Luckily, Carlo was early and was already waiting for them.

"Carlo," Jada shouted upon seeing him. "Who is Santa Priscilla and where is the Greek Chapel?" She showed him the text as Justin, sitting on the edge of a fountain, started searching frantically in his guidebook.

"Greek Chapel . . . Greek Chapel," Carlo mused. "Doesn't ring a bell. But the Catacombs of Saint Priscilla are an important religious, historical, and archeological site dating from late second century AD. Saint Priscilla was a Roman noblewoman whose husband was killed by Emperor Domitian for being a Christian. The ancient Romans persecuted and often killed people who practiced Christianity. Saint Priscilla created an underground burial place for the bodies of Christian martyrs that expanded to house over 40,000 bodies."

Catacombs

"So the catacombs are a huge underground cemetery," Jada exclaimed.

"Found it!" Justin chimed in. "The Greek Chapel is a domed room at the heart of the underground Catacombs of Saint Priscilla. The entrance to the catacombs is in a convent on Via Salaria. Is it far?"

"And can we get there by noon?" Jada added, checking her watch. It was 11:26.

"We can if we take my Vespa, but only one of you can ride with me," Carlo responded.

"You go, J," Justin said. "I'll take an Uber and meet you there. I can take your backpack."

Jada put on the helmet Carlo offered her, hopped onto the back of the Vespa, and they took off at top speed. Jada wrapped her arms tightly around Carlo's waist. They weaved in and out of traffic, but Carlo was as adept at steering the Vespa as he was at driving a jet ski. They arrived at the convent in fifteen minutes.

The hushed, cool calm of the chambers and corridors of the convent were a sharp contrast to the bright June sun, scorching heat, and noise of the streets of Rome. The nun who sold them their entry tickets to the catacombs told them that the first guided tour of the day would be in English and start at one o'clock, but Carlo explained that they preferred to explore the catacombs on their own. Admonished to follow the marked pathway and not deviate into any other passageways, Jada and Carlo headed down steep stone steps into the depths of the catacombs. The rough stone walls were sandy in color and left a fine dust on her hands when Jada touched them to keep her balance as they descended further and further underground.

They reached the bottom of the stairs and continued walking along a dimly lit corridor. There were countless other passages that were offshoots from the main path that led into total darkness. The walls on either side of corridor had rows and rows of holes, some shallow and some deep, and of varying lengths, carved into them.

"Did these holes used to hold the bodies?" Jada asked, peering inside of one.

"Yes. Most of them are empty now. The bones have been moved because tourists kept taking them as souvenirs," Carlo replied.

"That's disgusting," Jada shuddered.

"This is a huge underground maze spanning eight miles. We had better stick to the main path or we may never find our way out," Carlo said.

A sign with an arrow pointing straight ahead indicated that they were going in the right direction for the Greek Chapel. They reached a small chamber and cautiously entered.

The Greek Chapel felt like a church inside a cave. There were chairs in rows facing a lectern and candles in sconces attached to the stone walls. Above their heads, painted into the arches above a chamber within the chamber, were the remains of ancient frescoes depicting scenes from the Bible. On a sturdy wooden table in the left corner of the chamber was a large ceremonial urn made of silver. It was heavy and ornate, and incongruous with the simple rough furnishings of the ancient stone room.

"That must be it," Jada whispered, "the urn my *amica* told us about." She peered inside, then stuck her hand in and felt around. But the urn was empty. Carlo came over and slowly and carefully tilted the urn on its side to reveal a sheaf of papers in a plastic sleeve underneath. Jada pulled them out, and she and Carlo started leafing through them. "Transport documents," he whispered excitedly. "A parcel is to be transported by train from Rome to St. Petersburg, Russia. The train leaves this evening at nine o'clock from Termini Station." Jada took out her phone and started to take photos of the pages.

"Jada, hurry. It's 11:55," Carlo informed her, anxiously checking his watch. "We'd better get out of here."

"OK, just a sec. I want to see if I can quickly text these pictures of the first few pages to Commissario Ruffalo. The sooner she knows about the transport, the sooner she can organize her team to intercept it. Darn it!" Jada said. "The signal keeps going in and out. We're too far underground. I guess I have to wait until we are out of here."

Just then, they heard a clattering sound coming from the corridor outside the Greek Chapel. Someone was approaching and had dropped something that clattered apart on the stone floor. They heard a man's gruff voice utter what was undoubtedly a curse, though they couldn't make out the word. Jada and Carlo shoved the pages back under the urn and looked frantically around the chapel for someplace to hide. They ducked into the side chamber of the chapel, and crouched on the floor in opposite corners of the dark recesses of the room. Jada knew they couldn't be seen from the chapel, but if the person approaching decided to enter the side chamber, he would definitely spot them.

A hulking figure entered the doorway of the chapel, his outline filling the frame. *Ivan.* Jada recognized the scarred, tattooed man immediately. Ivan muttered angrily to himself. He had dropped his phone and was trying to put the case back on it. Jada and Carlo scarcely dared breathe for fear of giving their presence away. They waited anxiously, crouching in the dark as Ivan struggled to put the case onto his phone the right way.

*What an idiot!* Jada thought. She hadn't realized that Ivan was all brawn and no brains. *Probably makes him even more dangerous,* she thought with a shiver. Ivan finally figured out how to reassemble his phone, put it in his pocket, and surveyed the chapel. Jada and Carlo instinctively lowered their gazes as Ivan turned in the direction of the entrance to the side chamber, as if by not looking at him they could prevent him from feeling their presence. He soon spotted the urn in the corner of the chapel and grunted as he lifted it to reveal the sleeve of papers. He flipped through the papers briefly, then slipped them into his inside jacket pocket. Jada and Carlo were about to exhale as Ivan turned to leave the chapel, when an audible *swoosh* sounded from Jada's pocket. Her phone must have briefly caught a signal and the text message to Commissario Ruffalo had gone through! Ivan stopped in his tracks and almost imperceptibly sniffed the air like an animal sensing his prey.

# CHAPTER 13

Ivan turned and headed toward where the sound had come from—Jada crouching in the corner of the inner chamber. She steeled herself, ready to swing into action. She just wasn't sure what action she was going to take.

"Yoooouuuuuu!" Ivan hissed as he squinted into the darkness, recognizing Jada. Just then an object hurtled through the air, hitting Ivan in his right eye. In a David vs. Goliath moment, Carlo had hurled an iron candlestick with all his might at Ivan's head. Ivan had been caught unawares because he had only spied Jada in the dimly lit room, so Carlo's attack was a total surprise. Ivan staggered back, holding his eye. Jada and Carlo scampered past him, out of the chamber, and then out of the doorway of the chapel. They had a head start, but Ivan was like an enraged bull and charged after them down the main lit passageway, holding his eye with his right hand. Jada realized they would never make it to the stone steps leading out of the catacombs without him catching up to them, so the only option would be to lose him.

Jada took the next sharp right off the main passage and plunged into darkness. Instead of following her, to confound Ivan, Carlo took the next left off the passageway. Jada walked as quickly and stealthily as she could in the pitch-black darkness. She didn't dare turn on the flashlight app on her phone for fear of giving away her location. The passageway she was in was not straight like the main one, but twisted and turned and spawned offshoots in both directions. Jada wished she could use GPS or even the compass function on her phone, but neither worked effectively underground. She even wished for a low-tech option like Hansel and Gretel's breadcrumbs to help her track her path, but her pockets were empty.

After a few minutes, she decided to stop going further into the maze for fear of becoming hopelessly lost inside. Jada sank down onto the ground to stop and think for a moment, but as soon as she sat she heard heavy footsteps. The catacombs had a cavelike quality that seemed to distort sound. Jada couldn't get a real sense of how close the footsteps were to her. Rather than risk running into Ivan in an attempt to get away from him, Jada decided her best option was to stay put but hidden. She felt along the wall for the nearest indentation, measured it with her hands, and judged it to be long enough. As the footsteps seemed to get closer, Jada climbed quietly inside the open crypt. The stone beneath her was cold and damp, and she suppressed a shiver. She saw a dim light from afar flicker and then go out, and then flicker again and then go out. *Ivan must be trying to use his phone's flashlight, but it's damaged,* she surmised. She slowly scooted sideways, further into the crypt, as the footsteps got louder and the sound of labored breathing got closer.

Ivan was clearly lost in the maze of the catacombs as well. Unfortunately for Jada, he stopped to get his bearings at exactly the same spot she had and was now standing just outside the crypt where she was hiding. If she reached out her hand she could touch him. She shrank back and all but held her breath. Ivan was breathing heavily, and when he doubled over in pain from his wounded eye, his head was level with the crypt in which Jada lay rigid with fear. Ivan bellowed like a wounded animal with rage and frustration. Jada smelled the onions on his breath, and she shrank back even further in revulsion. His long primal scream seemed to calm him a bit, and after sighing deeply, emitting more oniony stench, he lumbered on in search of the exit.

Jada waited until she could no longer hear him, and then she waited five minutes more, counting the seconds in her head. She decided she had to risk being detected and use the light from her phone to try to find her way. She couldn't stop the scream that escaped her when she illuminated the crypt. She was not alone. Lying next to her was a skeleton about the same height as she was. Its head was turned toward

Jada, its mouth open as if in a silent scream back at her. Its teeth were broken off and partially missing, and empty eye sockets stared unseeing into Jada's eyes. A few strands of long dark hair still stuck to its skull and fragments of cloth clung to the body. Jada clambered quickly out of the crypt and started running to get away from the spooky bones. Jada rounded a corner and ran full throttle right into—Carlo!

"Thank goodness it's you," she cried, relieved. "For a second I thought I had bumped into Ivan."

"It would have—how do you say?—*sucked* to bump into the very person you were running away from," Carlo responded, grinning, clearly very happy to see her and pleased to have used a slang word in English.

"Actually, I was running away from someone else," Jada said and told him about the skeleton.

"Ah, so that's why you screamed," Carlo replied. "It's a good thing you did because I never would have found you otherwise. I was headed the other way until I heard you, and I doubled back in the direction I thought your scream had come from. I think I know how to find the main passageway. This way."

They took off by the light of Jada's phone until they could see the dim light of the passage leading to the stairs in the distance. They heard a voice in English and realized the tour must have started. They hung back until the 1:00 p.m. tour group had passed, then emerged from the side passage and made their way to the stairs and out. Justin was waiting for them on a bench outside the convent. He reported seeing a hulking guy emerge from the convent, clutching his eye before jumping on a Vespa and speeding away.

# CHAPTER 14

"Are you sure you can get us in?" Jada asked Carlo worriedly. After they filled Justin in on their run-in with Ivan in the catacombs, Jada and Carlo returned to the scene of the crime, the museum. They wanted to see if they could pick up any additional clues and ask a few more questions of Marco Vitti, the assistant director of the museum who had been interviewed by the police.

"I know the receptionist from when I worked here last summer. I can get us in," Carlo assured her. They strode purposefully up to the information desk in the entrance hall of the museum. Carlo spoke to the receptionist in rapid-fire Italian, pausing only to punctuate whatever he was saying with a charming smile. The young receptionist, who looked to be in her late teens at most herself, twirled her hair and hung on his every word. Jada feigned interest in a museum brochure while Carlo plied his charms, but kept one eye and one ear on his conversation with the flirty receptionist.

After what seemed like ages of chitchat Jada couldn't decipher, the receptionist whispered, "*Si, si. OK,*" and escorted them to the door to the museum's administrative offices. The girl gave Jada a challenging stare as she held the door open for them, which Jada coolly returned as she walked past.

"Charm will get you far in this town," Jada commented to Carlo when they had gone in.

"That and connections," Carlo responded. "My grandfather is a trustee, and our family have been benefactors of the museum for

decades. The receptionist knew the museum director would have
allowed us in, but I still had to make believe she was doing me a favor,"
he winked at Jada. "She passed on an interesting bit of information,"
Carlo continued. "Vitti has disappeared."

"What?" Jada was shocked. "When?"

"He didn't turn up for work two days ago and hasn't responded to
calls or visits to his home," Carlo replied. "His wife has no idea where
he went." It was lunchtime, and except for the tapping of a keyboard
behind a closed door at the end of the corridor, everyone seemed to
be out. They entered the office with a plaque outside that said *"Marco
Vitti"* without encountering a soul.

"Doesn't seem like he left in a hurry," Jada commented, noting how
neat and orderly the office was. The shelves were lined with books in
alphabetical order by author, and his files were bound in file folders
grouped by color. "Vitti wears glasses, doesn't he?" Jada asked, peeking
inside his desk drawers.

"Yeah, he used to joke that he was blind as a bat without them.
Why?" Carlo asked.

"No glasses here. Not even a spare pair in a desk drawer. In fact,
there are no personal items in this office whatsoever. Was it always this
sterile? Do you remember if Vitti kept any personal objects in here?"

Carlo thought for a moment. "He is a huge football—I mean, soccer
fan," Carlo recalled. "His team is called *Lazio,* and he used to have a
ball signed by the team on the table over there." Carlo pointed to an
empty side table. "He also used to hang the team scarf on the coat rack
by the door. I remember because we used to joke about soccer all the
time when I worked here. I support *Roma*, a rival team to *Lazio*."

"So," Jada said, "when Vitti left here last, he took items of great
sentimental value with him. Doesn't sound like someone who has met
with foul play or an accident. Sounds like the actions of someone who
was leaving and not intending to return." Jada sat down at Vitti's desk
and turned on his computer. "Drat! We need a password to get into the
system."

"I know the password for interns, but it wouldn't get us into Vitti's
files. Wait a minute. His password was *laziopersempre. Lazio* always. I

remember I had to use it a few times when I was working on a project for him. Being a *Roma* supporter, it always galled me to type those words."

"How do you spell that?" Jada asked. Carlo came over and stood behind her at the computer. He reached his arms around her and typed the password into the keyboard.

"Password incorrect! He must have changed it," Carlo said, defeated. Jada typed. *Ding*! "I'm in."

"What was the password?" Carlo asked, surprised.

"I added a 1," Jada responded.

"Of course!" Carlo said, slapping his forehead. "*Laziopersempre1*. *Lazio* always number 1—the logical next password for Vitti. Jada, you are brilliant!"

"Thanks," said Jada, warmed by Carlo's compliment. "Now let's see what Vitti was up to before his sudden disappearance." Carlo pulled up a chair next to Jada, and together they trawled through Vitti's files. One called "*Minacce*" caught Carlo's eye. "What does it mean?" Jada asked.

"Threats," Carlo responded, scrolling through the file. "There are at least fifteen unsigned letters to Vitti scanned into this file. Most of them are from ten years ago, but the last three were received more recently, about six months ago."

"What do they say?" Jada asked.

"They are mostly insulting, calling Vitti a liar and a thief, and threatening to expose and ruin him. The thing is, they are not really specific, so I can't tell what the author of these rants is so angry about," Carlo responded.

"Wow, so Vitti was being threatened and harassed. These letters could be valuable evidence." Jada took a flash drive from her backpack, and Carlo downloaded the file onto it. Next, they checked Vitti's browser history. "Mumbai, Beijing, Moscow—looks like Vitti was planning to travel abroad, judging from these travel websites he visited," Jada said.

"The question is, is Vitti travelling alone or is he carrying some very important cargo with him?" Carlo wondered.

"And is he running away from someone and not just from the law?" Jada added. "Strange, he researched airline tickets to each of those places, but it doesn't look like he actually bought any, at least, not with this computer. I wonder if he has a laptop or other devices we should try to get a look at. Maybe we should give Commissario Ruffalo a call."

Jada whipped out her phone and dialed the *commissario*. She relayed to the detective where she and Carlo were and what they had found. "Jada, you and Carlo really shouldn't be snooping in Vitti's office," Commissario Ruffalo said sternly and paused, "but . . . I was just about to request a warrant to search Vitti's office as well as his work computer, and your detective work has saved me the trouble. I can now deploy my officers directly to his home. His wife has declared him a missing person, so we can search his home as part of that investigation, though I have to say his disappearance has raised his profile as a suspect in the missing scepter case."

"What about tonight's train?" Jada asked. *If Ivan and Vitti were working together,* Jada thought, *maybe the plan was to transport the scepter by freight train while Vitti would fly and meet the cargo in Russia.*

"Unfortunately, I doubt the transport will go ahead as planned since the culprits know we are on to them," Commissario Ruffalo answered. "I plan to have my people stake out Termini Station tonight just in case, but I'm not hopeful we'll succeed in intercepting anything. The good news is that thanks to your intervention, the scepter is likely still in Rome, so we have a much better chance of finding it."

Jada was thankful for the *commissario*'s kind words, but she couldn't help think that if she and Carlo hadn't been discovered by Ivan in the catacombs, the transport at Termini Station would have gone ahead as planned, and intercepting the scepter there would have been possible.

"Any leads from the first few pages of the transport documents I sent you?" Jada asked.

"The recipient is a Russian shell company. It is likely owned by another company, which is owned by another—like the famous Russian *Matryoshka* nesting dolls. My team is investigating to figure out who is the ultimate owner, but it may take a while. Unfortunately, since both the freight fee and customs duty were paid in cash, there is no way to shortcut the investigation by following the money, as we would have if the payments had been by check, wire transfer, or credit card. We are clearly dealing with professionals here, Jada," Commissario Ruffalo said. "And if Vitti is involved, he is not working alone."

# CHAPTER 15

The next day, Jada entered the shiny modern glass-and-steel office building that housed the Boroni headquarters on the outskirts of Rome. She wanted to talk with someone inside the company about the Boroni glove found at the crime scene. Jada's father was usually willing to help with her detective work and had arranged for her to meet with the Boroni head of research and development. Given that Mr. Johnson would be his boss if the merger went through, it was not surprising Enrico Mattoni agreed to the meeting.

A receptionist escorted Jada to the elevator, which they rode to the basement. They exited and walked down a long, empty hallway with closed doors on either side. It was eerily quiet and was missing the usual buzz of an office. There was no hum of printers, no voices on conference calls, no ringing of telephones, no sign of life at all. "Is everyone on vacation?" Jada asked the receptionist.

"No, no," she replied. "This floor is used mainly for storage. Signor Mattoni has the only office here." They took a right turn, and at the end of the hallway at the back of the building was a door with a nameplate reading "*enrico mattoni*" in all lower-case letters.

"Signor Mattoni, thank you so much for meeting with me." Jada shook hands with the prematurely balding, slightly stooped man whom she had last seen covered in tomato soup in the Boroni cafeteria. He ushered her into his cramped office after thanking the receptionist, who practically fled back to her post in the spacious, airy main lobby. The one small window in the office had a view of the garage. Piles of documents on the floor formed pillars of paper, and reports and books covered every surface.

"Please call me Enrico. And please excuse the mess," Enrico said, removing a pile of papers from a chair so Jada could sit down. He stepped over a box of Boroni advertising materials to squeeze behind his desk opposite Jada.

*What a tiny office for someone with such a senior position in the company,* Jada thought. The only part of the office that was neat and orderly was the bookshelf behind Enrico's desk, which was filled with fossils and ancient pottery fragments, stone and iron tools, and remnants of jewelry. Jada remembered that Anna Conti had told her that Enrico had almost completed a degree in archeology. "I'm sure my father told you that I am looking into the case of the missing scepter of Maxentius."

"He did," Enrico replied, "and at first I was surprised a girl your age would tackle such a thing, but your father filled me in on some of your previous sleuthing successes. I very much like to encourage young people to pursue their passions, so I told him I would be happy to be of assistance, if possible. How can I help with your investigation?"

"Well, Signor Mattoni . . . I mean, Enrico," Jada said. "I have found a clue linking the crime scene with Industria Boroni. A green latex glove of the type worn exclusively by Boroni factory workers was found in the museum the night the scepter was stolen." A look of surprise came over Enrico's face. "Do you know of anyone connected with the company who might have a motive for stealing the scepter?" Enrico thought for a moment, then he shook his head.

"I guess if I had to be honest, Jada, I would say that I am the only person I know with any interest, other than a monetary one, in the scepter. The scepter is the archeological find of the century. Any archeologist would kill to have made the discovery. And any collector would love to have the scepter as the centerpiece of his or her collection. At the risk of putting myself under suspicion, I honestly don't know anyone else at Industria Boroni with an appreciation of the importance of the scepter."

The phone rang and Enrico cringed slightly when he saw the extension number that came up on caller ID. "I'm sorry, I have to take this," he said, picking up the phone and swiveling his chair so that his back was to Jada. Jada could hear the other voice on the line as clearly as if it were on speaker phone since the caller was screaming so loudly. She couldn't decipher the rapid-fire Italian, but she could tell Enrico was being told off in a big way. "*Si, si,* Giovanni," he sighed into the phone in a shaky voice. "*Subito*" was his final word, but the loud click of the caller hanging up could be heard before he could get it out.

"I'm afraid you'll have to excuse me, Jada, but I have to end our discussion here," Enrico said, jumping to his feet and frantically gathering papers from his desk. "An urgent matter has come up, and I have to meet with the CEO, Giovanni Boroni, *subito*, right away. I believe he is currently in conference with your father and other representatives of your father's company. I'll walk out with you."

Papers in hand, he escorted Jada to the elevators and pushed the call buttons numerous times. Enrico seemed relieved when the express elevator to the executive suites on the top floor arrived first. He shook Jada's hand then hopped on the elevator, but as the door was closing, he stuck his arm out to open it again. "If I were you, Jada, I would focus on the money. There are very few people who have an interest in ancient artifacts. They are not like paintings you can hang on your wall for all to admire. I would bet your thief had a purely financial interest in the scepter, which is worth millions. Now, if you'll excuse me, Giovanni is waiting." He bowed his head in resignation as the elevator door closed, and he headed up to what was certain to be another in a long line of very unpleasant meetings with the CEO.

# CHAPTER 16

Jada went back to the lobby, where an attractive dark-haired woman in her late twenties was waiting for her. She was dressed stylishly in a pencil skirt, chic silk blouse, and sky-high stiletto pumps. "Hello, my name is Maria Carla Morelli, and I am the personal assistant of CEO Giovanni Boroni. You must be Jada," she said in lightly accented English.

"Yes. Pleased to meet you," Jada responded.

"Mr. Johnson said you would be meeting him here to go to lunch. Unfortunately, his meeting with the CEO and management is still going on in the conference room. They should be done shortly, though. Would you like to wait in the CEO's office?" She escorted Jada up to a large top-floor office. Two entire walls were made of glass, providing a panoramic view of the city in the distance. Giovanni's desk was a long rectangular glass table supported by metal sawhorse legs. The wall behind his desk was covered with framed photos and clippings from newspapers and magazines.

"Have a seat. Can I get you anything while you wait?" Maria Carla asked as Jada settled onto the couch in the sitting area opposite Giovanni's desk.

"No, thanks," Jada replied.

"Well, I'll get back to work," Maria Carla said. "If you need anything, I'll be just in the next room." She referred to the antechamber outside the office housing her desk and workstation that they had passed through on their way in. Maria Carla closed the door, and a minute later, Jada could hear her chatting on the phone. Jada soon got bored and wandered over to the glass wall to admire the view. She then spotted a photo of her favorite soccer player and Giovanni on the wall behind his desk, and went over to examine it more closely. The wall was a tribute to Giovanni's jet-set lifestyle. Giovanni on his private plane. Giovanni on his father's yacht. Giovanni at fashion shows, awards ceremonies, and fancy parties. There were pictures of him with celebrities and sports stars, famous chefs who used Boroni products, politicians and business leaders, actors and supermodels, and his favorite soccer team. Jada noted sadly that although Giovanni's wall was covered with photos, there wasn't one of Carlo.

There was one man who appeared in photos with Giovanni more frequently than anyone else. Boris Blatov, according to a framed newspaper article on the wall featuring a picture of him and Giovanni ice fishing on a lake in Siberia, was a Russian oligarch worth over fifty billion dollars. On a hunch, Jada tapped his name into her phone so she would remember it.

Jada turned around and looked at the piles of documents and reports littering Giovanni's desk. She didn't hear Maria Carla's chatter anymore, but Jada listened closely and heard the sustained clicking of the assistant's keyboard. She decided to have a peek at the papers. One document caught her eye because it was not in Italian or English, but in the Cyrillic alphabet. Jada couldn't be sure but it seemed to be written in Russian. It looked like some sort of agreement. And under the signature lines were the names The Blatov Group and Industria Boroni, in English and in Italian.

Jada noticed that the clicking outside the door had stopped. She turned away from the desk to face the wall of photos just as Maria Carla opened the door. "Oh," said Maria Carla, slightly surprised not to find Jada on the couch where she had left her. "I see you are looking at the CEO's photos. He is a very busy man." Jada thought she detected a hint of sarcasm in Maria Carla's voice. It would be normal for a head of a major company like Industria Boroni to be busy with work, but Jada noted that most of the photos showed Giovanni at play.

Jada smiled innocently and said, "I see Giovanni Boroni knows Alessio. He's my favorite soccer player. He has an amazing left foot. And he's *so* handsome too." She could see Maria Carla relax now that she had an explanation for why Jada was behind Giovanni's desk.

"I brought you some Italian fashion magazines. Do you like clothes?" Maria Carla asked.

"*Molto*. Very much." Jada said, trying out an Italian word. She went back over to the couch and started flipping through one of the magazines Maria Carla had placed on the coffee table. Just then Maria Carla's phone rang in the next room. She rushed to answer it, closing the door behind her.

"*Amore*," Jada heard Maria Carla exclaim, and she hoped Maria Carla would have a nice long romantic chat with her love on the other end of the line. Jada took her cell phone and tiptoed back over to the desk. She opened the Russian document and started taking pictures of each page. She would email them to Lauren, her father's assistant in the US, to see if she could get them translated. Jada was a few pages from the end of the agreement when she heard the door to the outer office where Maria Carla sat open and her dad and Giovanni's voices in heated discussion.

"I'll need the research and development team to give me the projections for the new product launches," Mr. Johnson said.

"We won't have that information for at least another month. They are still doing their preliminary market testing on two of the three new product lines," Giovanni responded testily.

Just as Jada thought she would have to stop photographing and miss getting a record of the entire agreement, Maria Carla interrupted Giovanni, seeming to ask her boss a question. Jada heard Giovanni reply to her in a condescending tone, clearly annoyed at her interruption. As he droned on in a voice one would use with a small child, Jada quickly photographed the final pages of the document, grateful for her father's good manners. She knew he would never enter someone else's office ahead of him, and in fact, Mr. Johnson had waited patiently while Giovanni instructed Maria Carla before following Giovanni into his office. Jada slipped the document back into the pile just as the door opened, and she whipped around to face the photo covered wall. Her dad and Giovanni found her standing behind Giovanni's desk, cell phone in hand, taking a picture of the photo of him and Alessio.

"Hi, Dad. Hi, Signor Boroni." Jada greeted the two men cheerfully. "I hope you don't mind," she said, smiling shyly at Giovanni, "but I love Alessio. My friends won't believe I've met someone who is his close personal friend." Giovanni puffed with pride at mention of his celebrity connections.

"Not at all," he replied. "I will get an autographed photo of him for you and send it to you through Carlo. That is, if I can trust that feckless boy to get it to you. My son seems to have trouble handling even the simplest task. Kids can be quite irresponsible, am I right, Johnson?" Giovanni said.

Mr. Johnson cleared his throat, and as on most matters, disagreed with Giovanni. "From what I've seen and from what Jada tells me, Carlo seems like a fine young man."

"An autographed photo would be great! Thank you," Jada interjected to change the conversation and hopefully end it. She clutched her phone and almost held her breath until she and her dad said their goodbyes and left Giovanni's office.

# CHAPTER 17

Piazza Navona

"Giovanni told me that Da Lorenzo is his favorite restaurant in Rome," Mr. Johnson told Jada as they sat down for lunch at a table covered in crisp white linen. They were in a roped-off area outside the front of the restaurant, separated from the hustle and bustle of tourists but directly on the square. Piazza Navona is a large square in Rome, built on the site of an ancient stadium, from which it takes its long rectangular shape. It is home to three beautiful fountains. The center of the square is full of tourists, street vendors, and artists who paint portraits and caricatures. The perimeter of the square is lined with cafés and restaurants.

"He and I may not see eye to eye on business matters, but I've had a few lunches with him and he knows his food. I'm sure we are in for a treat."

"The menu says they use only Boroni pasta," Jada noted.

"The chef is internationally renowned and is a close personal friend of Giovanni," Mr. Johnson added.

"He seems to have a lot of close personal friends who are famous. Did you see the wall of fame in his office?" Jada giggled.

"I did," her dad replied. "After dealing with him in negotiations, I looked for a picture of him with Lucifer himself. We are having a devil of a time negotiating the deal in which AmeriFoods will buy Industria Boroni. His father, Augusto, is fully on board, but Giovanni seems to be doing everything in his power to slow down the deal. I'm beginning to wonder if he's not two-timing us and negotiating to sell to another company. There have been some rumors in the market about another international company interested in Boroni."

"The rumored other company wouldn't be Russian, would it?" Jada asked.

"Why, yes. One of the rumored competitors is a Russian conglomerate. How did you guess that?" Mr. Johnson asked, putting his menu down and gazing intently at Jada.

"Well, when I was in Giovanni's office, I happened to notice a document in Russian on his desk."

Mr. Johnson raised an eyebrow. "You happened to *notice?*"

"Weeelll . . .," Jada began, hoping her dad wouldn't be angry that she had been snooping.

His curiosity got the better of him, and rather than chastise her, he asked, "What kind of document was it?"

"I don't know," Jada responded. "It was in Russian, but the names Industria Boroni and Blatov Group were in Italian and English. It seemed like some sort of agreement. I took pictures of the document and sent them to Lauren for translation."

Mr. Johnson's assistant had worked for him for over fifteen years and had known Jada since she was a baby. She was like a beloved aunt to the Johnson children. She would often help Jada on her "cases" and joked that she had two bosses, but she would never reveal which one was her favorite. She would wink at Jada when she said this, and Jada's dad would laugh and say that he knew where he stood.

"The Blatov Group, the company owned by Boris Blatov, the Russian billionaire, is one of our rumored competitors. Jada, you may have found proof that the rumor is reality," Mr. Johnson exclaimed.

"Giovanni Boroni seems to be besties with Boris Blatov, judging from the number of pictures with him he has up," Jada commented. "Let's see what we can find out about Mr. Blatov," she continued, taking out her phone and typing his name into the search bar of her web browser. "According to Wikipedia, Boris Blatov is one of the five richest men in Russia. In addition to being a businessman, he is an avid hunter, fisherman, skier, and art and artifact collector, with one of the biggest private collections of antiquities outside of major museums."

Mr. Johnson whipped out his cell phone and sent a text to Lauren: *"Translation Jada requested urgent."*

Lauren responded immediately: *"Work already underway. At a minimum, description of document due from translation service within the hour."*

"Enough time to have a nice lunch," Mr. Johnson said as they tucked into their pasta.

After a fantastic meal finished off by tiramisu for Mr. Johnson and a mountain of ice cream for Jada, father and daughter decided to take a stroll around the *piazza*. As they stopped in the middle of the square at the Fountain of the Four Rivers, Jada started to feel queasy. She wondered if maybe four scoops of ice cream had been too much. "Dad, I don't feel well," she managed to say before her stomach started to heave. Luckily, a garbage can was nearby, and Jada managed to get the lid off just in time to deposit inside the entire lunch she had just eaten. In an instant her dad was by her side, handing her his handkerchief and patting her back. Jada wiped her mouth and marveled that what was such a pleasure going down could be so foul coming back up.

They sat down on a bench for Jada to catch her breath before going in search of a taxi. Various hawkers tried to sell them souvenirs or offer to paint their portrait, but Jada's dad waved them away. "I think I can make it to the taxi stand now," Jada said. She turned to her dad and found him head bowed, sweating profusely and trembling.

Just then a cart pushing souvenir vendor they had refused earlier came back over to them for another try. "T-shirt. Baseball cap. All say 'Roma.' Ten euro. Just ten euro," he shouted.

"No, thank you," Jada said firmly.

"Come, girl!" the hawker insisted. "You very pretty in this hat. Mister," he continued in his broken English, turning to Mr. Johnson, "get little girl souvenir of Rome. Very cheap. Only eight euro," he said, dropping the price to try to make a sale. Mr. Johnson looked up weakly. Jada tried to shoo the man away, but he wouldn't budge. He pushed his cart right up to Mr. Johnson's knees, blocking him from getting up and leaving. He pulled a T-shirt from the pile and spread it out on top of the cart so Mr. Johnson could get a good look. "Five euros!" he announced. Mr. Johnson's mouth contorted and to the shock and horror of the vendor, he started to retch and heave. The vendor couldn't react quickly enough. He tried to pull back the cart, but it was too late. Mr. Johnson had thrown up all over the T-shirt and many of the other souvenirs in the cart. Mr. Johnson stood shakily as the vendor cursed and shouted over his ruined goods. Mr. Johnson managed to take out his wallet from his pocket and hand it to Jada. "Give him all the euros in there," he told her. Jada pulled out a wad of bills.

"Dad, there's about three hundred euros here," she said. Mr. Johnson motioned for her to give it to the vendor. On receipt of the money, the vendor calmed down. He dumped the heavily soiled T-shirt in a garbage bin and declared most of the other souvenirs salvageable. He called over a friend to watch his cart and escorted Jada and her dad to a nearby taxi stand and helped them in. It was a good thing he helped them, because Jada wasn't feeling well again.

She leaned back in the taxi seat and said to Mr. Johnson weakly, "Do you think someone could have deliberately given us food poisoning?"

"I don't think so, Jada. Who would do such a thing? Everything tasted delicious, but maybe my fish wasn't as fresh as I thought it was."

"I had the beef, Dad. In fact, we each had different pasta dishes too. You don't like to share so there was no overlap in what we ate, yet we both got sick."

Mr. Johnson shook his head weakly, but Jada could tell he was considering her theory. "I know there could have been cross contamination of the cooking utensils, but for some reason I have a sinking feeling our getting sick was no accident," Jada surmised.

She and her dad were able to make it back to the hotel without any more "accidents," but they spent much of the evening and night kneeling on the marble floor of the bathrooms of their suite. It wasn't until the next morning that Jada felt better and checked her cell phone to find a text message from Lauren: *Document translation summary—Company Sale and Purchase Agreement.*

# CHAPTER 18

Pantheon

"A lot of beggars hang out at the Pantheon, so maybe we can find Rosela here," Carlo told Jada as he locked his Vespa with a chain to an iron gate. They took off their helmets, and Jada hoped she didn't have hat hair. They were in Piazza della Rotonda, a large square in the heart of Rome that housed the famous ancient church, the Pantheon. They hoped to find Rosela again to see if they could get more information on Ivan, the tattooed man who they were sure was connected to the theft of the scepter, and to see what else she might know.

The square was bustling with Romans out for a stroll, tourists visiting the main attraction of the church, and street vendors selling their wares. Jada took a picture of Carlo in front of a fountain and then a few more shots of the square for the scrapbook she was making of her trip to Rome.

A couple kissing in a corner was a quintessentially Roman scene, and Jada couldn't help snapping a pic of them. The woman had on staggeringly high wedge-heeled sandals, super skinny jeans, and a cute tank top with sparkly sequins on the shoulder straps. She was sort of dressed up for a Saturday afternoon and way too glamorous for her partner, who was shorter than she, and judging him from behind, rather nondescript looking. Jada zoomed in on the glamorous woman's face and then let her camera drop. Luckily it was on a strap around her neck. "Hey," she nudged Carlo, who was standing next to her admiring the obelisk. "Isn't that your dad's secretary, Maria Carla?" she asked him. When Carlo turned to look, the couple had stopped kissing and was walking arm in arm out of the *piazza*. Jada was amazed at how sure-footed the woman was in high heels on slippery smooth cobblestones.

"*Mamma mia!*" Carlo said. "I think it is."

So Maria Carla was on an afternoon date with her *amore*! They couldn't get a good look at him since the couple was on the opposite side of the square and the man's back was to them the entire time, but he was definitely not the tall, dark, and handsome type Jada would have expected a fashionista like Maria Carla to go for. *Love is blind*, Jada thought.

"Good for her. Glad she has a life outside of the office since working for my father can't be easy. It certainly isn't easy living with him." Carlo frowned for a second, then seemed to shake off the negative thought. "Let's go in the church for a minute. Before we stake out the square, I want to show you something cool inside the Pantheon," he said.

As suggested by the name Piazza della Rotonda, the Pantheon is round, with curved walls, and covered by a massive dome with a hole in the middle. The oculus in the ceiling is open and provides the only source of light to the interior of the building as well as a startling view of the sky. Carlo took Jada's hand and led her into the center of the group of tourists staring upward. Then to Jada's surprise, he lay down right in the middle of the floor directly underneath the hole in the dome and motioned for her to lie next to him. "You'll get a great picture from here," he said, grinning. Jada joined him and took the best photo of her trip that didn't include Carlo. After they got up, other tourists scrambled to the ground to get the same shot of the dome with its window to the sky.

They left the Pantheon and sat on the curved wall outside the building to chat and scour the crowd for any sign of Rosela. Jada hesitated before asking, "Carlo, what did you mean when you said your dad is hard to live with?"

Carlo paused before answering, and Jada could feel him debating whether to open up to her. He must have decided he could trust her, because he sighed and began, "I know my dad can be a harsh boss at work. But I also know how much he wants Industria Boroni to be successful, and how much pressure he's under because of current financial difficulties. He's stressed at work, then he brings the stress home with him and sometimes takes it out on me. He gets angry easily and he's super critical. Nothing I do or say is good enough for him. Maybe it's not such a bad thing that since my mom died he seems to find reasons be at home as little as possible. Let's just say he has a lot of social commitments as well as work ones."

"I'm so sorry," Jada said. "At least you have your grandparents in your life."

"*Nonno* and *Nonna* are great. They are like parents to me. In many ways, I'm really fortunate."

Not sure what to say, Jada took Carlo's hand in hers, and his warm squeeze back let her know it was exactly the right response.

A group of beggars entered the square and started approaching tourists, asking for money. Then Jada noticed a familiar figure at the edge of the *piazza*. Rosela, the girl who had tried to steal her backpack, was begging, bringing one hand to her mouth to mime food and holding one cupped hand out to ask for money. "Carlo, look," Jada said. "Northeast corner of the square. Do you see her?" They dropped hands and hopped down from the wall to head over to Rosela, who was talking to a female tourist. "Let's approach carefully," Jada said. "We don't want her to get spooked and run."

The tourist took pity on the scrawny girl in tattered clothes and put some coins in her hand. Rosela pocketed the coins and was about to approach another group of tourists nearby, when a large late-model black SUV with tinted windows pulled up at the end of a street that led onto the *piazza*. Its horn beeped, and Rosela turned and ran over to it. Before Jada and Carlo were halfway there, the back door of the SUV opened, Rosela hopped in, and the car did a U-turn and zoomed away.

"Any chance that Rosela has a rich uncle who wants to take her out for ice cream?" Jada asked as they stood in the middle of the square watching the car disappear down the narrow road.

"More likely a rich employer," Carlo replied.

# CHAPTER 19

"OK, we're nearly there. Just fifty meters more. Step up here. The ground is a bit uneven. I got you." Carlo guided a blindfolded Jada with directions, one hand around her waist and the other holding her hand as if they were couple skating. It was her tenth day in Rome, and Carlo had said he had a surprise for her. The only hint he had given her about where they might be going was that she needed to wear a swimsuit.

"*Ecco!*" Carlo announced as he removed the blindfold, unveiling the most idyllic scene Jada had ever laid eyes on. They were at a lake with sparkling deep green water, surrounded by a forest of tall oak and chestnut trees. The sky was an azure blue dotted with fluffy white cumulus clouds. The grassy shore of the lake turned to charcoal gray sand as it met the water. "Lago di Martignano," Carlo announced, telling her the name of the lake. He held her hand and escorted her to a red and white checked tablecloth laid out on the grass with a picnic basket on top. An attendant brought them two lounge chairs and then discreetly slipped away.

"Carlo, this is great. We have the entire beach to ourselves. How did you manage to do this?" Jada asked.

"Being a Boroni has its privileges," Carlo said with a wink. They sat down on the ground, and Carlo took a wireless speaker from his backpack and played Italian pop music softly in the background. It felt a little bit like Christmas as they opened the picnic basket to discover the delicious treats inside—all Boroni products, of course. They lunched on tiny mozzarella balls; little salami bites; a cold pasta with cherry tomatoes, basil, and olive oil; and a salad of rucola, parmesan, and bresaola—all washed down with Jada's favorite *aranciata*. Dessert was a slice each of *crostata*, a thin pie made of crumbly crust baked with a thick layer of blueberry jam.

"Wow, I am so stuffed," Jada said when they had finished. "I really do need to wait half an hour before swimming."

"That's just a—what do you call it?—old wives' tale," Carlo said. "I know a great way to work off a big meal." He changed the playlist to American hip-hop and cranked up the volume. "Shall we dance?" he asked, hopping to his feet and formally holding out his hand to Jada. Jada hesitated for a moment, but then her curiosity and the music got the better of her; she stood up, and they danced. Carlo was good. His moves were practiced, but he had the rhythm and timing of someone for whom dancing came naturally. He was up on most of the latest American dances thanks to music videos, but Jada had fun teaching him a new move or two. He followed her with ease, and then a slow song came on and it was her turn to follow him. They swayed together in the shade of the trees, surrounded by beauty, and Jada knew she would remember this moment always.

"I have another surprise for you," Carlo said as the song ended. "Do you know how to scuba dive?"

"I've been a couple of times on vacation with my family, and I absolutely love it," Jada responded, "but I'm not certified or anything."

"This is a shallow dive, so certification isn't required. I'll just run through the basics with you before we go. This lake is sixty meters or about two hundred feet deep at the center. It is a little less than a mile across. It used to be a volcano, which is why the sand is almost black since it is essentially ground volcanic rock. Anyway, in ancient times the water level here was much lower and the shoreline was much farther out. Just ten meters under the water over there," Carlo said, pointing to the right side of the lake, "are the ruins of an ancient Roman nobleperson's house. It used to lie on the shore of the lake, but now it's submerged. I thought we would take a look."

"Let's go," Jada said eagerly. They went to the shed of the attendant who had brought them the lounge chairs and got scuba gear. The attendant gave them masks and flippers and helped Jada strap on her vest and oxygen tank. Carlo reminded her of the basics of breathing. She put in the mouthpiece of her oxygen regulator, and they were off. The fresh water of the lake had a smooth, velvety feel that was very different from ocean water. It was also murkier than salt water, and the floor of the lake was covered in tall algae. Fish darted in and out of the wavy green fronds. Jada thought she saw an eel, which made her squeamish. But they were swimming away from it, so she put it out of her mind and paddled on.

The water was opaque with sediment, so Jada had to concentrate to follow Carlo. She was grateful he was wearing bright yellow swimming trunks. They swam down through the murky depths, and as they descended, the water became clearer and colder. After paddling for a while, they spotted the outline of a stone structure. It was the villa. Carlo used his underwater torch to illuminate a rectangular opening that must have been a window. He stopped, and they both peered inside. Carlo motioned at the window with his index finger. Then he made the thumbs-up gesture, followed by the thumbs-down one. Did they dare to enter? Jada thought for a second, then gestured thumbs-up. Carlo copied her, then he took the lead, lighting their path with the flashlight.

They entered a small room, and Carlo shined the light around. The floor was covered in a thick carpet of algae. Protruding from the green vines in the corner was a large object that looked to be made of terra-cotta. They swam over to investigate it. It was a broken vase lying on its side, and algae was growing inside of it. Carlo pointed the torch at the wall, and fragments of color caught in the beam of light. The wall was partially covered in mosaic tiles. The colors had faded and some of the tiles were broken, so they were unable to tell what the mosaic had once depicted, but it was a stunning discovery nevertheless. Despite the years that had passed and the toll being submerged had taken, it was clear that this house had once been beautiful.

There was a large rectangular hole in the left corner of the room that was probably a doorway, and they swam over to peer into the dark depths that lay behind it. Despite the torch, they couldn't see very well inside. Carlo shined the light on the pressure gauge of his oxygen tank and then held up his fist to Jada, a signal that he had a quarter of a tank left. He shined the light on hers and she had about the same. They looked at the doorway, then at each other, and Jada shook her head. They had no idea the size of the villa, there was very little light, and it would be disastrous to get lost inside a possible labyrinth of rooms and then run out of oxygen.

Carlo pointed the flashlight at the window through which they had entered, and they swam toward it. Carlo went through, but as Jada was passing through behind him, her foot got tangled in something and she was stuck. Thinking it was algae, she tugged her leg. Not only did her foot not budge, but she felt something cold and metal clamp onto her ankle. Jada pulled with all her might but the metal ring around her ankle was attached to something immovable. She squinted behind her scuba mask and noticed fronds of algae underneath on the lake floor parting in a line away from her. Jada knew the creature swimming away was no fish. Carlo realized she was no longer behind him and doubled back to find her half out of the window, half inside the house. He signaled for her to follow him, and she frantically motioned downward to her foot. Carlo shined the light to find that around her ankle was a rusty metal ring attached to a chain. He swam down into the forest of algae to discover the chain was attached to a metal ball twice the size of a large bowling ball. Jada had been manacled to the floor of the house. Carlo handed Jada the light, and he pulled on the chain as hard as he could, but the ball was immovable. Jada put the light on the window ledge so they could both pull with two hands, but the ball barely budged. It would take three or four strong people to lift the weight.

Jada grabbed the light again and checked her oxygen gauge. She was now at an eighth of a tank. She showed her gauge to Carlo and saw his eyes widen in alarm. He mimed to her "a little bit" using his forefinger and thumb and then pointed away. She didn't know what his plan was, but at least she knew he was coming right back. Jada didn't want to waste oxygen, so she didn't try to pull anymore, but she did test each link of the chain to see if there were any weak ones. The chain was rusty but sound. Carlo came back carrying a rock and began pounding at the chain. Jada was still, but her mind was whirring. She had an idea, and if it worked, she would have her mother to thank.

She swam down to Carlo and tapped him on the shoulder, motioning for him to stop banging. The bracelet part of the manacle was loose on her ankle but wouldn't fit over her foot. She pulled off her right flipper and pointed her toes as hard as she could, causing her heel to retract a little. She was able to start easing the ring down, rusty metal scraping her skin. As she continued, it felt as if the top of her foot and her heel were being crushed by a vise, but finally she was able to pull the ring off, taking off a layer of skin from the side of her foot with it. Carlo grabbed the flashlight and they swam out and up, both holding their last inhalations from their oxygen tanks. They broke the surface of the water, ripped the useless mouthpieces from their mouths, and gasped for air. Jada's foot was scraped and bleeding, she had lost a flipper, but she was free. She silently thanked her mother for the genetic gift of slim ankles and narrow feet, as well as for the years of forced ballet lessons.

# CHAPTER 20

Corner of the Four Fountains Statue

Jada and Carlo sat in a cozy corner of a café in Rome, sipping hot chocolate and brooding over the near miss at the lake. The hotel doctor had bandaged Jada's foot, and she had it elevated on a chair.

"I can't believe that the person who tried to kill you got away," Carlo fumed. "I didn't even get a glimpse of him."

"Or her," Jada added. "The water was murky and the algae was thick. We had very little visibility, Carlo, and more importantly, very little oxygen. Please don't beat yourself up."

Just then, she heard the distinctive *boing* of her phone. Someone had sent her a Snapchat. She checked her phone, expecting to see a friend making a silly face on her screen, but instead the image of a stone figure reclining sideways greeted her. The figure was propped on her elbow, head resting on her fist, and she was dressed in draped garments. That's all Jada could note before the image from an unknown sender disappeared.

"Who is it?" Carlo asked, noting Jada's puzzled expression.

"I don't know who sent it. It was a picture of a statue." Jada described the statue to Carlo, but he couldn't identify it.

"I've been thinking about Marco Vitti and where he might have disappeared to," Carlo said. "I remember overhearing a number of heated arguments over the phone between him and his wife last summer when I was working at the museum. After one really bad argument, he slammed down the phone and said that if it weren't for his job, he would move back to Sicily."

"Vitti was from Sicily? I thought he was from Rome," Jada said.

"He is, but I think his grandparents were Sicilian. The Sicilians take their bloodline very seriously. If you have Sicilian blood, you are Sicilian, no matter where you were born."

"I wonder if Vitti still has family in Sicily. Do you have an online phone directory here?" Jada asked. "Ours is called the White Pages." She picked up her phone and opened the web browser.

"Ours is too. *Pagine Bianche*," Carlo replied. He spelled out the letters as Jada tapped it into a Google search.

"There are twelve Vittis in Sicily. It may be worth trying to figure out if any are related to him," Jada said. "I'll text Commissario Ruffalo to tell her about the Sicily connection."

"Of course, the Sicilians are well known for another reason," Carlo said.

"Mafia," Jada responded. "Do you think . . .," Jada began, but she was interrupted by the *boing* of another Snapchat coming through.

This time Jada was ready. She took a screenshot of it and showed it to Carlo. This statue was of a man, also reclining on his side, but his arm was down and he was holding a cornucopia. He wore draped clothing like the first statue, and a lion peeked out from behind him. Stalks of tall plants in bas relief decorated the panel behind him, and they reminded Jada of the algae in the lake at Martignano. "This statue looks familiar. I know I've seen it before," said Carlo, "but I can't place it."

He didn't have long to ponder because two more Snapchats came in quick succession, and Jada was able to screenshot both of them. They were of two more reclining stone statues, one male and one female, but these had more ornamental backgrounds than the first two. On closer inspection, all of the statues were the backdrops for a fountain. Jada pointed this out to Carlo, and it jogged his memory. "Four fountains," he said. "The corner of the Four Fountains is an intersection in the center of Rome. I must have passed through it a hundred times on my Vespa, but I've never stopped to take a good look at them."

"Someone wanted to bring them to our attention. Let's go check them out," Jada said.

"This may be a trap, Jada. We need to be alert," Carlo said.

"Always," Jada replied.

They approached the corner of the Four Fountains on Carlo's scooter. They decided to pass through the intersection once to scope it out before looping back to visit it on foot. Traffic was slow and heavy, so both Jada and Carlo were able to survey the crowd of mostly tourists standing on the corners taking pictures, and neither noticed anything amiss. Carlo locked the Vespa a block away, and they walked back to the intersection, Jada limping slightly on her bandaged foot. She went to examine the two fountains on one side of the intersection, while Carlo took the two on the other side. Jada took out her phone and pulled up the Snapchat photos so she could compare the statue in the photo to the real thing. Maybe there was a clue tucked into the stonework that the photo would reveal. Jada noticed nothing unusual. She crossed the street to examine the other fountain on her side, but there was nothing noticeable there either. She looked across the street at Carlo, and he looked at her and shrugged his shoulders to tell her that he too had found no clues.

Jada stepped back to take a photo of the fountain whose picture she had not been fast enough to take a screen shot of, and that's when she noticed it. Lining the base of the fountain on the ground were individual pieces of pasta in a chainlike row. They were shells, which was consistent with the water theme of the fountain and the statue, but they were definitely a recent addition to the artwork. She picked a couple up, went back to the other fountain, and sure enough, the pasta pieces were there as well. Jada crossed the street to Carlo and opened her hand to show him what she had found. "*Conchiglie?*" he asked, surprised. "Shells," he translated. The base of his fountain was lined with the little pasta shells as well, as was the fourth fountain on his side of the street.

"What does it mean?" Jada asked, perplexed.

"I don't know," Carlo said, "but I can tell you this, these shells are smaller than most pasta of this type. Only we make *conchiglie* this small. This is Boroni pasta."

# CHAPTER 21

Trevi Fountain

It was 6:00 a.m. when the distinctive *ding* of a WhatsApp message on her phone woke Jada up. At home, her parents didn't allow electronic devices in the bedroom after bedtime, but on vacation she was allowed to use her phone as an alarm clock. She reached over to grab it from the nightstand next to her bed, sleepily wondering if it was from a friend who didn't realize there was a six-hour time difference between home and Italy.

*Three coins in the fountain*
*Will bring you lots of luck*
*Read the writing up above*
*Don't worry if you get stuck*
*Doesn't matter it's in Latin*
*The words don't count at all*
*If the letters become numbers*
*They will tell you whom to call*
*18-10-16-10-5-8*
*20-8-17-2-8-10*

*———Un amica*

Jada bolted upright in bed. The message wasn't from a friend at home, but from her "friend" here. She immediately forwarded the message to Carlo and Justin, then jotted down "early riser" on the list of traits of her *amica* in her notebook. She found her guidebook on Rome on the coffee table of the living room of their suite. There were so many fountains in Rome, but when Jada arrived at the page with a picture of the iconic Trevi Fountain, she knew it had to be the one.

Completed in 1762, the Travertine marble fountain stands eighty-six feet high and a hundred and sixty-one feet wide, and is the largest Baroque fountain in Rome. Even though it is made from solid marble and stone, the scene depicted is one of turbulent water. Legend has it that if you make a wish while throwing coins in the fountain, using your right hand over your left shoulder, facing away from it, your wish will come true. Jada examined the photo in the guidebook, and sure enough, there was an inscription above the fountain. She had to get there and check it out herself. It wasn't too far from the hotel; her parents would probably let her take a taxi. Jada showered and dressed quickly. As she was arranging her hair in a topknot, her phone pinged with a message: "Trevi Fountain. I'm waiting downstairs on my Vespa. Carlo."

Ten minutes later they had the fountain to themselves, since it was too early in the morning for most tourists and for all but a handful of Italian early birds on their way to work. "CLEMENS XII PONT MAX AQUAM VIRGINEM COPIA ET SALUBRITATE

COMMENDATAM CULTU MAGNIFICO ORNAVIT ANNO DOMINI MDCCXXXV PONTIF VI," Carlo read the inscription over the fountain out loud.

"Is that Italian? What does it mean?" she asked, curious even though her *amica*'s message had said the meaning of the words didn't matter.

"It's Latin, and it's basically a dedication of the fountain by Clemens the twelfth, the pope who commissioned it in 1735," Carlo replied. *"They will tell you whom to call,"* he read aloud from the message of the *amica*. "But the numbers that follow are definitely not phone numbers, at least not in Italy."

Jada reached into her backpack and took out a notebook and a pen. She wrote down the inscription, carefully spacing the letters. "What if we assign a number to each letter in the order that it appears in the inscription. Like this."

| C | L | E | M | E | N | S | X | I | I | P | O | N | T | M | A | X | A |
|---|---|---|---|---|---|---|---|---|---|---|---|---|---|---|---|---|---|
| 1 | 2 | 3 | 4 | 5 | 6 | 7 | 8 | 9 | 10 | 11 | 12 | 13 | 14 | 15 | 16 | 17 | 18 |

| Q | U | A | M | V | I | R | G | I | N | E | M | C | O | P | I | A | E |
|---|---|---|---|---|---|---|---|---|---|---|---|---|---|---|---|---|---|
| 19 | 20 | 21 | 22 | 23 | 24 | 25 | 26 | 27 | 28 | 29 | 30 | 31 | 32 | 33 | 34 | 35 | 36 |

| T | S | A | L | U | B | R | I | T | A | T | E | C | O | M | M | E | N |
|---|---|---|---|---|---|---|---|---|---|---|---|---|---|---|---|---|---|
| 37 | 38 | 39 | 40 | 41 | 42 | 43 | 44 | 45 | 46 | 47 | 48 | 49 | 50 | 51 | 52 | 53 | 54 |

| D | A | T | A | M | C | U | L | T | U | M | A | G | N | I | F | I | C |
|---|---|---|---|---|---|---|---|---|---|---|---|---|---|---|---|---|---|
| 55 | 56 | 57 | 58 | 59 | 60 | 61 | 62 | 63 | 64 | 65 | 66 | 67 | 68 | 69 | 70 | 71 | 72 |

| O | O | R | N | A | V | I | T | A | N | N | O | D | O | M | I | N | I |
|---|---|---|---|---|---|---|---|---|---|---|---|---|---|---|---|---|---|
| 73 | 74 | 75 | 76 | 77 | 78 | 79 | 80 | 81 | 82 | 83 | 84 | 85 | 86 | 87 | 88 | 89 | 90 |

| M | D | C | C | X | X | X | V | P | O | N | T | I | F | V | I |
|---|---|---|---|---|---|---|---|---|---|---|---|---|---|---|---|
| 91 | 92 | 93 | 94 | 95 | 96 | 97 | 98 | 99 | 100 | 101 | 102 | 103 | 104 | 105 | 106 |

"What do her numbers spell out?" Jada asked. Carlo read each number of the code, and Jada wrote the corresponding letter under it:

| 18 | 10 | 16 | 10 | 5 | 8 |
|----|----|----|----|---|---|
| A  | I  | A  | I  | E | X |

| 20 | 8 | 17 | 2 | 8 | 10 |
|----|---|----|---|---|----|
| U  | X | X  | L | X | I  |

"Gibberish in English," she sighed. "Does it mean anything in Italian or Latin?"

"'*Ex*' in Latin means 'out of' or 'from,' but the letters before '*ex*' have no meaning. The bottom row could be numbers in Roman numerals if it weren't for the U. No, Jada, it makes no sense." Carlo shook his head. They both stared in confusion at the letters and numbers. Suddenly, Jada turned the page in her notebook and started furiously scribbling the letters of the inscription again.

"What if each letter's number is unique and repeats when the letter repeats?" she asked, thinking out loud.

| C | L | E | M | E | N | S | X | I | I | P | O | N | T | M | A | X | A |
|---|---|---|---|---|---|---|---|---|---|---|----|----|----|---|----|---|----|
| 1 | 2 | 3 | 4 | 3 | 5 | 6 | 7 | 8 | 8 | 9 | 10 | 5 | 11 | 4 | 12 | 7 | 12 |

| Q | U | A | M | V | I | R | G | I | N | E | M | C | O | P | I | A | E |
|----|----|----|---|----|---|----|----|---|---|---|---|---|----|---|----|----|---|
| 13 | 14 | 12 | 4 | 15 | 8 | 16 | 17 | 8 | 5 | 3 | 4 | 1 | 10 | 9 | 8 | 12 | 3 |

| T | S | A | L | U | B | R | I | T | A | T | E | C | O | M | M | E | N |
|----|---|----|---|----|----|----|---|----|----|----|---|----|----|---|---|---|---|
| 11 | 6 | 12 | 2 | 14 | 18 | 16 | 8 | 11 | 12 | 11 | 3 | 1 | 10 | 4 | 4 | 3 | 5 |

| D | A | T | A | M | C | U | L | T | U | M | A | G | N | I | F | I | C |
|----|----|----|----|---|---|----|---|----|----|---|----|----|---|----|---|---|---|
| 19 | 12 | 11 | 12 | 4 | 1 | 14 | 2 | 11 | 14 | 4 | 12 | 17 | 5 | 8 | 20 | 8 | 1 |

| O | O | R | N | A | V | I | T | A | N | N | O | D | O | M | I | N | I |
|----|----|----|---|----|----|---|----|----|---|---|----|----|----|---|---|---|---|
| 10 | 10 | 16 | 5 | 12 | 15 | 8 | 11 | 12 | 5 | 5 | 10 | 19 | 10 | 4 | 8 | 5 | 8 |

| M | D | C | C | X | X | X | V | P | O | N | T | I | F | V | I |
|---|---|---|---|---|---|---|---|---|---|---|---|---|---|---|---|
| 4 | 19 | 1 | 1 | 7 | 7 | 7 | 15 | 9 | 10 | 5 | 11 | 8 | 20 | 15 | 8 |

Carlo read the code again, and Jada assigned each number a letter according to her new key:

| 18 | 10 | 16 | 10 | 5 | 8 |
|----|----|----|----|----|----|
| B | O | R | O | N | I |

| 20 | 8 | 17 | 2 | 8 | 10 |
|----|----|----|----|----|----|
| F | I | G | L | I | O |

They stared at the letters in disbelief.

"*Figlio* means . . .," Jada began.

"Son," Carlo finished her sentence. "I may be a Boroni son, Jada, but I assure you I have nothing to do with any of this."

Jada thought for a second and said quietly, "I think in this case, Carlo, the son might be your grandfather's son, your father."

Carlo sat down on the edge of the fountain as that realization sank in. "I know my dad can be really difficult. And when it comes to business, he is known for being quite . . ." Carlo searched for the right word in English. "Ruthless," he continued. "But I don't want to believe he could be involved in criminal activity." Carlo put his head in his hands in despair.

Jada had been wanting to tell Carlo about his dad's plan to double-cross her dad and sell Industria Boroni to the Blatov Group instead of AmeriFoods, but she knew the news would be devastating to him. Also, evidence that Giovanni could be dishonest in business dealings didn't necessarily mean he was capable of criminal behavior. "Let's not jump to any conclusions," Jada said. "The message just says he is the person to call. Can you talk to your dad and ask him what he might know about the scepter's disappearance?" Jada avoided using the word "theft."

"Jada, he would bite my head off if I asked him something like that," Carlo said, shaking his head.

Jada nodded sympathetically. Just then her phone vibrated. "Voicemail," she said, checking the screen. "I forgot I had my ringer off.'" As Jada listened to the message, her eyes widened with excitement. "It was Commissario Ruffalo," she reported to Carlo when she was done. "There has been a breakthrough in the case. The police found Marco Vitti in Sicily, and are bringing him in for questioning."

# CHAPTER 22

Ponte Milvio

Later that evening, Jada relaxed in the hotel suite, waiting for her parents to return from the opera. Her phone rang and her face lit up when she saw the name CARLO on her screen. "You'll never guess who just called me." Carlo's voice crackled and the line went dead. Jada waited and ten seconds later her phone rang again.

"Who?" she asked.

*Crackle, crackle, static.* "—la," Carlo answered.

"Who?" Jada shouted.

"Just a mo—" *Crackle, crackle . . .* "Up on deck," Carlo responded. A few seconds later he asked, "Better?"

"I hear you now," Jada responded. "Who called you, and where are you?" she asked.

"Sorry, I'm on the *Fuga.* The network is not very strong out at sea. I'm up on the deck now. My dad is having a party, and apparently my attendance is required because the crew is short-staffed. He is busy wining and dining some business associates, and I have to help serve the food and drinks. Dinner is almost over, so I have to hurry before he starts yelling at me to clean up."

"Poor you! Wish I were there," Jada said, and then felt her cheeks go hot after speaking with such feeling.

"Me too," said Carlo softly, and Jada blushed even more deeply.

"Who called you?" Jada asked, more sharply than she had intended, overcompensating for her previous tone.

"Rosela, the Roma girl who gave you a run for your money," Carlo laughed, pleased he had made a joke in English.

"*Ha-ha.* What did she say?" Jada asked.

"Well, she wants to meet with you and *only* you. She says Ivan contacted her again, and she has information on his whereabouts. She asked if you could meet her at Ponte Milvio, a bridge over the River Tiber, at 10:00 p.m. Oh, and she wants one hundred euros, cash. Do you have that much money?"

"Luckily, I haven't bought too many souvenirs," Jada responded. "That's most of my spending money for this trip, but I have it."

"I don't know about this, Jada. It could be a set-up. She was a bit too insistent that you come alone. She claims what she has to give you doesn't need translation. I want to come with you, but I'm stuck on the boat until late tonight from the looks of things. Should you contact the police?" Carlo asked.

"I've already left Commissario Ruffalo a couple of messages after receiving her voicemail this morning. She must be busy because she hasn't called me back. I hate to bother her with this in case it turns out to be a useless lead or just a ploy to make some money," Jada responded. "I know, I'll ask Justin to go with me. He'll remain at a distance so she doesn't get spooked, but close enough that he can keep an eye on the situation."

"Sounds like a good plan," Carlo responded. "Promise me you won't change your mind and go alone?"

"I promise," Jada said, softness creeping into her voice again, her cheeks burning again.

Jada Googled *Ponte Milvio* to find a map of the area, and was surprised to learn it was the site of an epic showdown between Emperor Maxentius and Emperor Constantine. Maxentius may even have been carrying his scepter as he rode into the battle at the bridge. By the fourth century AD, the Roman Empire was divided into two parts: the eastern empire, with its capital in what is now Istanbul, Turkey; and the western empire, with Rome as its capital. Emperors Constantine and Maxentius jockeyed for power and control of the western empire, and eventually Constantine decided to oust Maxentius and rule the western empire by himself.

On October 28, 312 AD, a definitive battle was fought between the two western emperors and their troops at Ponte Milvio. Constantine reportedly saw a vision prior to the battle that promised him victory if he fought with the symbol of Christ on his shield. Constantine proved to have the upper hand in military strategy, and Maxentius made the fatal mistake of not positioning his troops so they would have a possible route of retreat. Maxentius' troops ended up attempting to flee to the other side of the Tiber over Ponte Milvio, which partially collapsed during the retreat. Maxentius himself ended up in the river, and drowned along with many of his men. His body was dredged up and decapitated, and the head paraded all over Rome as proof of his defeat.

It is believed that during or soon after the battle of Ponte Milvio, Maxentius' scepter was hidden, probably so it would not fall into the hands of Constantine. It remained undiscovered for nearly 1,700 years. Constantine's victory over Maxentius resulted in the conversion of the empire and its subjects to Christianity. Constantine later went on to defeat the emperor of the eastern empire, Licinius, and united the eastern and western empires under his sole control.

Jada and Justin asked the Uber driver to drive past Ponte Milvio a couple of times so they could scope it out. Above the entrance to the huge stone bridge was a tower building two stories high, which looked to be in disrepair from disuse. There were two arched doorways housing antique wooden doors on either side of the tower building. The bridge was for pedestrians only, and couples and groups of young people strolled along. They decided that Justin would sit at an outdoor restaurant across the wide boulevard from the bridge entrance, where he would have a good view of the meeting place but hopefully not be noticeable among the tourist and Roman diners. They got out of the taxi a few blocks from Ponte Milvio, with Justin getting into position at the restaurant first, and Jada approaching the bridge a few minutes later alone.

Jada stood for a few moments at the entrance of the bridge, but when Rosela didn't appear, she started to walk across it to see if she would run into the girl. Jada stopped halfway to gaze down at the green-gray water of the Tiber rushing below. She couldn't help but picture Maxentius and his men being swept to their deaths in the forceful current just below where she was standing. She shuddered, then continued toward the other side of the river.

With no sign of Rosela, Jada made her way back across the bridge. When she reached the tower building, she stood for a moment in its shadow and looked across the road to where Justin was keeping watch. To her dismay, her view of him (and his of her) was blocked by three peddlers who stood in front of his table, aggressively trying to sell him souvenirs.

"Psstt! Jah-da! Jah-da!" Jada heard her name, mispronounced. There in the shadows of the tower building was Rosela, calling her over.

"Rosela! I've been waiting for you. Do you have something for me?" Rosela leaned against the wooden door near the arch of the tower and held out a folded piece of paper. Jada wondered if it contained an address where Ivan could be found. She walked over to Rosela and extended her hand to take the paper, but Rosela abruptly snatched her hand back.

"Money," she whispered. "One hundred euros."

*So Rosela speaks some English after all,* Jada thought. She was reaching into her backpack to get the money to show to Rosela, vowing to herself not to pay until she had seen what was written on the paper, when suddenly hands grabbed her roughly from behind. The old wooden door they were standing next to, which looked like it had been shut for centuries, swung open and she was shoved inside. Jada opened her mouth to scream, but a calloused hand clamped over it, muffling all sound.

# CHAPTER 23

Jada's feet barely touched the stairs as she was spirited up three flights to the top of the bridge tower. The air was musty, and Jada could barely see in the unlit staircase and the dark room at the top. Rosela spoke to the man holding Jada. She couldn't understand the words, but Jada detected alarm and concern in Rosela's voice. Perhaps her abduction was not part of their agreement. The man responded gruffly in a few words of broken Italian. If Jada had any doubt as to who was holding her in his viselike grip, all doubt was erased once he spoke. She recognized the gravelly voice with the Slavic accent and the onion-laced breath immediately: Ivan. He ripped off her backpack and tossed it in a corner, then barked something at Rosela. Rosela hesitated, then reluctantly walked over to a wooden chest in the center of the room, unlocked it, and opened the lid. Jada was seized with panic as she realized Ivan's intention—he was going to lock her inside.

Jada struggled with all her might, but she couldn't break free from the granite arm wrapped around her. She opened her mouth as if to scream, but instead bared her teeth and bit down on the hand clamped over her mouth. She managed to catch a bit of the flesh of Ivan's palm between her teeth, and she chomped on it as hard as she could. Ivan howled in pain, but didn't let go. Jada felt a sharp pinch just above her collarbone near her neck, and everything went black.

When Jada came to, it took a moment for her to realize where she was. But once she did, she wanted to black out again. Heights she found thrilling, speed was exciting, but closed-in spaces were her Achilles' heel. Jada was claustrophobic, and she was now living out her worst nightmare. She was stuffed in a box the size of a small child's coffin, lying on her side with her knees pinned to her chest. It took all of her inner strength not to scream and howl. She tried to stop her heart from racing and to force her mind to calm down so she could think rationally. Freaking out would be futile. She had no idea how long she had been unconscious and didn't know if Ivan was still in the room. There was no telling what he would do to her when he found out she had regained consciousness, so she decided to be still and quiet.

Not moving and keeping quiet would also conserve oxygen. But wait—Jada noticed it was not entirely pitch-black inside the box. There was a circle of gray and chinks of gray here and there. They were cracks and holes in the antique wooden box, and the circle must be the keyhole. Jada was relieved to realize she wouldn't suffocate to death. Her left arm was pinned under her but her right arm was free, so she gently but firmly pushed upward on the lid of the box. As she suspected, it was shut tight, but she still felt a crushing disappointment that the lid had not budged.

A voice boomed outside the box. Ivan was there. Was he talking to Rosela? No, he was speaking in English. Jada couldn't hear Rosela, and she couldn't hear any response to Ivan. He was talking on his phone. Jada turned her head so she could listen with both ears. "*Da, da,* is all good," she heard him say in Bulgarian and English. "I have her and she's not going anywhere." There was silence as he listened, and then, "Look, Maria Carla, she was getting close and you say to me to get the situation under control. I took matters into my own hands, and it is now under control." His tone had turned to menacing anger in an instant. "Tell your boss merger meeting tomorrow morning is all his."

*Maria Carla . . . Merger meeting . . .* Jada thought. Ivan was talking to Maria Carla, Giovanni Boroni's secretary. And he was referring to tomorrow's meeting to vote on the sale of Industria Boroni to her dad's company, AmeriFoods. Jada's mind whirred at the implications of this new information. She *knew* the theft of the scepter and the merger deal were connected somehow. Jada heard a bang and then silence. Ivan had left, but she wasn't sure for how long. She had to figure out a way out of the box. Her phone was in her backpack, so she couldn't call Justin for help. The lid of the box was tightly shut. Jada pressed the sides of the box with her right hand and her feet as best she could to try to find a weak panel—to no avail. Despite the small chinks, the box was a solidly constructed antique. She would have had more luck with a modern chest from Ikea. Her only hope was to pick the lock. She had mastered the trick on her locker at school, and hoped an old-fashioned lock would work with the same mechanism. Jada's eyes welled with tears when she thought of the perfect tool for lock picking, her Swiss Army knife, in her backpack with her phone.

As she tried to shift into a more comfortable position, the topknot of her hair pushed against the side of the box. If she loosened her hair she would gain inches of space. Wait a minute—her thick hair was held in place by two super-strong bobby pins! It was painstaking work in the tight space, but using her right hand, Jada eased one of the pins out of her hair and inserted it in the lock. In trying to figure out the mechanism she pushed too far, and her heart sank when the bobby pin fell through the keyhole and onto the floor on the other side. Jada used her sleeve to wipe a tear of frustration from her cheek and beads of sweat from her forehead, then worked the other bobby pin out of her bun. After what felt like ages of trial and error, she felt a click. The lock turned. She pushed the lid up. The musty air of the dank, dark room felt like a mountain breeze compared to being trapped in the tiny box. She was free.

Jada grabbed her backpack from the corner of the room and dashed to the door, but when she tried to turn the heavy iron handle, it wouldn't budge. Jada was still locked in, but at least she was no longer crammed in a box. She paused and searched the dark room for another exit. There were no other doors, and she was too high up to jump out of the window. The room was pretty bare, and she found nothing she could use as a rope to lower herself down. Jada heard heavy footsteps on the stairs on the other side of the door.

She scanned the room, searching for something she could use as a weapon. The doorknob jangled as Ivan tried to open the door from the other side. There was a thud as he charged into the door to break through. Jada spotted a wrought-iron candelabra on a table in the corner. She grabbed it and stood to the side of the door, arm raised to lower it onto Ivan's head when he entered. The door was ancient but solid, and withstood the blows from the other side, but the hinges were starting to give way. With a mighty bang, the door came off its hinges and thudded to the floor. Jada opened her eyes, which she'd squeezed shut against the dust and splinters from the fallen wooden door, to find towering in the doorway . . . Justin!

"J, thank goodness I found you!" he cried, his voice full of relief, brow furrowed with worry. "Are you OK?"

"I'm fine," Jada said, giving her brother a big hug. "Thanks for breaking me out of here. It was a trap, and Ivan locked me in that box." She pointed to the small chest in the center of the room. "How did you find me?"

"Remember that family tracking app Mom and Dad made us install on our phones? The one we protested so much against getting as an invasion of our privacy? Well, it just came in handy," Justin replied.

"Yeah, I guess it did," Jada admitted. "Let's get out of here."

They left the bridge tower and went outside. Jada's eyes swept the bridge and the street, looking for any sign of Ivan or Rosela. There were still plenty of people hanging out and strolling around on the beautiful moonlit night, but no sign of her captors.

"Mom and Dad must be sick with worry about us," Justin said.

"I don't have any missed calls," Jada reported, checking her phone. "Do you?"

"Actually, neither do I," Justin said. "No texts either."

"Me neither. They probably came in late from the opera, saw our closed bedroom doors, and assumed we were sleeping. They don't even know we're out," Jada said.

"You're right, J."

"Which is good because we have someplace we need to go right now," Jada said urgently. "I'll call Carlo and see if he's back on land and able to meet us." Jada stuck out her hand and a cab swerved over to the curb to pick them up.

# CHAPTER 24

Carlo kissed Jada on both cheeks Italian style when he met her and Justin outside the front entrance of Boroni headquarters. "I'm so relieved you are OK," he said tenderly, and Jada smiled at his concern for her. He used his keycard to buzz them into the building, and then again to activate the elevator to the executive suite. They entered the suite marked *CEO Giovanni Boroni* and turned on the lights in Maria Carla's antechamber outside the office. Carlo tried to open the door to his father's office, but this time his keycard wouldn't grant him access.

"*Cavolo!*" he cried.

"*Cavolo?*" Justin asked.

"Cabbage," Carlo translated with a chuckle. "That's one Italian expression I can't explain, but you get the meaning: shoot, darn, drat. Anyway, I thought my card gave me access to the entire building, but I guess I was wrong."

"It's OK," Jada said. "This is the office I'm most interested in." She recounted Ivan's phone conversation while she was locked in the box, highlighting the bombshell news that he was taking his orders from Maria Carla. "We've got to get to the bottom of her relationship with Ivan, and I have a feeling we'll find an explanation somewhere here. Justin, you take the filing cabinet. Carlo, you search that closet and those bookshelves. I'll take her desk."

"What are we looking for?" Justin asked.

"I don't know exactly, but we'll know it when we find it," Jada responded.

The team worked diligently, but found nothing out of the ordinary. Jada went to open the last drawer in Maria Carla's desk and discovered it was locked. She searched the cups and containers on the desktop and the other drawers for a key, to no avail. She grabbed her backpack, took out her trusty Swiss Army knife, and got to work picking her second lock of the day. The lock clicked open, and Jada was disappointed to find a pile of magazines, some of which Maria Carla had offered her when she had visited Giovanni Boroni's office while waiting for her dad. There were a few fashion magazines mixed in with mostly business periodicals.

*She must keep these magazines for visitors who are left waiting for the very busy and important CEO,* Jada thought, closing the drawer. She thought again and reopened it. *Why would a drawer containing magazines be locked when all the others were unlocked?* Jada removed the magazines and stared at the empty drawer. She tapped the bottom and then pressed around the edges. When she put pressure on a spot at the bottom toward the front of the drawer, a lever was released and the wood came loose. The drawer had a false bottom.

"Bingo!" Jada said, as she pulled out a file that had been secreted in the drawer. Justin and Carlo stopped their search and joined Jada at the desk. Also in the drawer was a cellphone. Jada checked it and found all the text messages that had been sent to her as clues and the photos of the four statues sent to her via Snapchat. Maria Carla was her *amica*!

Thoughts whirled through Jada's mind. *If Maria Carla is trying to help me find the scepter, how can she also be instructing Ivan, who is trying to stop me? Is she acting on her own? On Giovanni Boroni's behalf? On behalf of someone else?*

The first document in the file folder was in Russian. It didn't seem like an agreement but more like a tax return or some other sort of government filing, but it had the names Industria Boroni and Blatov Group sprinkled throughout. She gave Carlo the fax number of her dad's assistant, Lauren, and he faxed her the document. Jada sent Lauren a text: *"Hi Lauren, Document on fax to you. Russian. Need translation urgently. Can you arrange?"*

*"You got it. Give me two hours,"* Lauren replied immediately.

The second document was a receipt for a bank wire transfer. "Five million euros," Justin exclaimed, reading over Jada's shoulder.

"I can't read the name of the sender because it's in the Cyrillic alphabet, but it's from a Russian bank," Jada noted, "to a Swiss bank. There's also no name for the recipient, just the account number."

"Some Swiss banks allow their clients to have anonymity," Carlo said. "It will be very difficult to uncover who received those funds."

"But I bet it's the initial payment for the scepter," Jada said, remembering the conversation she overheard at the Vatican between *Monsieur* Paul and Ivan. *Five million today, fifty million on delivery in St. Petersburg.* "Not only is Maria Carla my *amica*, but she is somehow involved with the sale of the missing scepter."

"But why would she be feeding you information on a sale she was trying to make happen? It doesn't make any sense," Justin questioned.

The other papers were transport documents relating to the export and delivery of a parcel. They were copies of the documents Ivan had collected in the catacombs. Now that they could examine them carefully, Carlo was despondent to see his father's signature on the last page on the line for the sender. "I guess I can't ignore the truth," Carlo said sadly. "My father must be responsible for the theft of the scepter." Justin patted him on the back, and Jada squeezed his hand. They checked Maria Carla's computer, but there were no emails other than work-related ones and the occasional personal exchange.

"Maria Carla must have communicated with Ivan and whoever else is involved only by phone," Jada said. "I wish I could have been a fly on the wall to hear her conversations."

"That's it!" Carlo cried.

"What is?" Jada and Justin asked in unison.

"We can be—how did you say?—flies on the wall for some of Maria Carla's calls," Carlo responded. Jada and Justin looked at him quizzically. "All of the phone calls at Boroni headquarters are taped, and the recordings are kept on file for thirty days before they are automatically deleted. It is a company policy to monitor employees that they are not told about. Only a handful of executives know about it. The recordings are only rarely accessed if an employee is suspected of behaving improperly. If my keycard gives us access to the communications and data room downstairs, and if my father hasn't changed my mother's name and birthdate as the password he uses for everything, we can listen to every conversation Maria Carla has had for the past month using the office phone."

"How much time do we have before the merger meeting?" Justin asked.

"It's 5:00 a.m.," Carlo responded. "We have three hours."

"Then we'd better start listening," Jada said.

They flew out of the door and down the stairs, not bothering to wait for the elevator. They collectively held their breath as Carlo placed his keycard on the electronic pad by the door to the data room. A green light flashed, the door clicked, and they were in. Rows of computers filled the room. Carlo sat down at a computer, and Jada and Justin sat on either side of him. He punched in the password, and the teens stared nervously at a dot pulsing in the center of the screen. All three cheered when the dot disappeared and a list of employee names and extensions populated the screen. He clicked on Maria Carla Morelli, ext. 2561. A list of dates and phone numbers came up.

"Let's start at the beginning," he said, clicking on the first call. With Carlo summarizing the content of the calls in English, they listened to a number of boring work-related conversations, interspersed with a few personal chats between Maria Carla and another assistant at the company in which they complained about their bosses. When the recording of the ninth call on the list began to play, the three teens leaned forward in their seats.

"*Amore . . .,*" Maria Carla's voice purred, her tone most definitely not businesslike.

"*Bellissima, cara mia,*" a voice familiar to Carlo responded to her, and Carlo stood up in shock at the sound of it.

* * * * * * * * *

Once Carlo had recovered, he translated the message and the ones that followed for Jada and Justin. After they had listened to all the taped calls, the three teens sat in stunned silence. Justin was the first to ask the obvious. "What do we do now?"

"First, we call Commissario Ruffalo and tell her everything," Jada responded, picking up her phone and dialing the *commissario's* personal cell number. She answered on the second ring. Jada put her phone on speaker so that the three of them could recount the details of the documents they had found and the messages they had heard to the *commissario*. The *commissario* then filled them in on the testimony of Marco Vitti to the Sicilian police as well as the discovery of the ownership of the Russian shell company that was buying the stolen scepter.

"Stay where you are," the *commissario* instructed. "I'm assembling my team and we are heading over. It sounds like the merger meeting will be the perfect opportunity to apprehend our suspects. Don't move, and let the authorities take it from here."

Jada hung up the phone and drummed her fingers anxiously on the table. "I'm worried about the merger deal going ahead. Our dad is counting on getting the deal signed this morning so that AmeriFoods can buy Industria Boroni. Something tells me that, based on what we've found, the deal is in peril."

"The meeting is about to start. Maybe we should go talk to my grandfather now," Carlo suggested.

"The *commissario* told us to stay put," Jada reminded him.

"What if we sneak up to the conference room and listen from outside?" Justin suggested. "Technically that's staying put because we haven't left Boroni headquarters."

"We don't have to go anywhere to listen in on the meeting," Carlo responded. "We're in the communications and data room. There's a surveillance system here that, if I can figure out how to turn it on, will let us see and hear what's going on in the conference room. Let's just say my dad sometimes finds it useful in dealing with counterparties on business deals to leave the room for them to discuss things 'privately.' In reality, he is listening in on everything they say from here." As he spoke, he sat back down at the computer, pulled up a program aptly called "007," typed in his dad's password, and video of the conference room came up on the screen. An assistant was placing documents on the table as Mr. Johnson walked into the room.

"Wait, we don't have audio," Justin commented.

Carlo moved the cursor on the screen to adjust the volume, and Mr. Johnson's voice giving instructions came through loud and clear. "Now what?" Carlo asked.

"We gather all the evidence we've uncovered, we watch, and we wait," Jada answered.

# CHAPTER 25

By 8:00 a.m., every seat at the long mahogany table of the main conference room at Boroni headquarters was taken. The merger meeting to approve the purchase of Industria Boroni by Mr. Johnson's company, AmeriFoods, was about to begin. At the head of the table sat Augusto Boroni, and next to him his two siblings and his nephew, Enrico Mattoni. The other chairs at the table were occupied by AmeriFoods representatives and members of the senior management team of Industria Boroni. Anna Conti, the manager of the primary Boroni factory, was in attendance, as was Maria Carla Morelli, secretary to the conspicuously absent Giovanni Boroni, CEO of Industria Boroni.

Mr. Johnson stood at the front of the room and called for attention. He requested the lights be dimmed and his assistant projected a presentation titled "AmeriFoods Inc. Acquisition of Industria Boroni" onto the whiteboard on the conference room wall. "Ladies and gentlemen," he began, "you will see on pages one and two of our presentation data you are familiar with. Sales at Industria Boroni, as well as revenue and profit, are falling, and have been for some time."

His assistant clicked the computer mousepad and a new page showed on the screen. "Page three shows the burden of debt the company is under after the arguably unnecessary expansion of its manufacturing facilities." He paused for effect before continuing. "Without an immediate infusion of cash into the business, you will be forced to sell assets, reduce production, and take an action I know is most unacceptable to you—firing a significant number of employees." After going through the charts and graphs in the rest of the presentation, Mr. Johnson nodded and his assistant turned off the projector and flipped the lights back on.

Mr. Johnson took off his glasses and addressed the Boroni family and management. "We at AmeriFoods would like to be the solution to Industria Boroni's problems. If you accept our offer to purchase the company, you will have the cash to pay off all of its debts, after which you, its current shareholders, will each receive a large cash payment. In addition, the job security of your workers will be ensured."

As Mr. Johnson spoke, his assistant handed out agreements and pens to the Boroni family members. "In summary," he concluded, "I ask you to sign the agreement in front of you because our acquisition of Industria Boroni is a win for all."

"Don't be so sure," a venomous voice shouted as Giovanni threw open the door and stormed into the room. Everyone looked up, startled at the unexpected interruption.

Augusto, pen poised over the signature line of the AmeriFoods acquisition agreement, looked up, pushed his glasses down to the edge of his nose, and addressed his son. "Giovanni, what do you have to add to these proceedings? And please continue to speak in English so our friends from AmeriFoods will understand you," he asked in a weary and annoyed voice.

"I only wish to add, Papa, that you do not have to turn over control of the business your grandfather built from nothing and that has been run by our family for four generations to these . . . *Americans*," he replied, practically spitting out the last word. "Your beloved son has found a buyer who will provide the money necessary to pay its debts and allow us to remain in control. We will restore Industria Boroni to its former glory as the premier pasta-making company in all of Italy!"

"What buyer have you found, Giovanni, and what will they pay? May I remind you that we are nearly 300 million euros in debt, thanks to you," Augusto said.

"I'm fully aware of the extent of our debt, Papa, and they will cover every penny," Giovanni responded. "The Blatov Group has made us an offer," he cried, waving an offer letter in the air, "that beats the

Americans' deal, and guarantees I will remain CEO so the Boronis remain in control of the company."

"How do we know," Augusto asked, "that the Blatov Group will allow the company to remain true to its values, to continue to produce a superior product and to safeguard the jobs of our loyal employees? You would remain CEO, but as the sole shareholder and owner of the company, the Blatov Group would be in control."

"Do you take me for a fool, Papa?" Giovanni shot back. "I have the assurances of my close personal friend Boris Blatov that I will be given a free hand to continue running the company."

Giovanni placed an agreement for the sale of the business to the Blatov Group in front of his father on top of the AmeriFoods agreement. "Papa," he said, his tone becoming gentle and persuasive, "this deal is far better for our company and our family than the American deal. I love Industria Boroni with all my heart as you do. I know I have made mistakes in the past, but give me another chance to prove to you that I can uphold the honor and legacy of the Boroni family. Trust me that selling to the Blatov Group is the right thing to do."

Augusto sighed heavily, clearly swayed by the sincerity and emotion his son had displayed. A battle was raging between his head and his heart.

"May I say something?" Enrico Mattoni cleared his throat and addressed his uncle.

"What could you possibly have to add?" interrupted Giovanni, but Enrico held up his hand to silence him.

"I want to add, cousin, that I agree with you. The Blatov deal is in my view a better solution for our company. Therefore, I too will vote my shares in favor of this agreement. I am ready to sign," Enrico said.

Giovanni's expression of surprise at his cousin's support for the Blatov deal transformed into a smirk. Without being bullied, Enrico was making it easy for Giovanni. Augusto Boroni turned his astonished gaze back and forth between his nephew and his son, whose views were aligned for once. After a long pause, hand shaking, he picked up his pen once again, this time to sign the Blatov agreement.

# CHAPTER 26

"Stop! You're making a big mistake," a female voice interrupted. All eyes again turned to the conference room door as Jada burst in, followed by Carlo and Justin. Jada had a document in her hand, Carlo carried Jada's backpack, and Justin carried a cardboard box with the Boroni logo on it. Jada's hair, loosened from its usual bun, was a black cloud around her face and shoulders. Her clothes were wrinkled and smudged with dust. Despite the ordeal she had suffered, and even after staying up all night, Jada's eyes shone like fire.

"Jada!" Mr. Johnson gasped. "What happened to you? And what are you doing here?"

"I'm fine, Dad, but we have some important information you all need to hear," Jada replied. She turned to the Boronis at the head of the table and placed a document in front of them. "This is a translation of a document the Blatov Group was required to file with the Russian government to obtain approval to purchase Industria Boroni. It details its exact plans for Industria Boroni once it owns the company, including changing the source of the wheat for the pasta from Italy to Russia, firing half of the Boroni workforce, and removing Giovanni as CEO and replacing him. It also states the intention of the Blatov Group to . . ." Jada picked up the document and began reading, "'Sell off the non-core assets of Industria Boroni to extract maximum value from the company.'" She placed it back on the table in front of Augusto.

"They plan to break up the company?" Augusto cried.

"Sometimes a company is worth less than the sum of its parts, so another firm will buy it and make a huge profit by selling it off piece by piece," Mr. Johnson explained.

Giovanni strode over to his father and picked up the document Jada had presented him. "This is certainly a fake produced by that girl and her father," he yelled, shaking the pages in his raised hand.

"The document is real, Papa," Carlo cried, squaring his shoulders and standing up to his father. "I was with Jada when she discovered it," he continued more quietly but firmly. Giovanni stared hard at Carlo, his eyes bulging with anger.

Before Giovanni could lash out at Carlo, Augusto silenced the room. "Enough!"

Augusto turned to his sister and whispered in her ear. He then spoke quietly to his brother and his nephew, Enrico. "I think," Augusto said slowly to Mr. Johnson, Jada, and the rest of those assembled in the room, "that the senior members of the Boroni family need to have a private meeting to discuss matters. We need to determine all of the facts before making any final decision."

Augusto stood up, took the document out of his son's hand, and waved him away with it. "I'm afraid this is one meeting to which you are not invited, Giovanni," he said. Giovanni glared at his father, his face beet red with rage. There was tension in the room as everyone waited for an explosive outburst. But after a beat, Giovanni turned on his heel, walked deliberately to a seat at the opposite end of the conference table, and sat down.

"Augusto, sir, you and your family members and fellow shareholders do need to have a discussion, but there is another important piece of information you are missing and another family member you may wish to exclude from your deliberations," Jada spoke calmly and forcefully. "I am sorry to report to you that Blatov's planned replacement for Giovanni as CEO of Industria Boroni is your nephew, Enrico Mattoni, who is also the thief of the ancient scepter of Maxentius."

# CHAPTER 27

There were gasps, murmurs, and whispers as some of those in attendance translated Jada's words into Italian.

Enrico visibly paled and stiffened in his chair, as still and white as a marble statue. Augusto looked sharply at him, but Enrico didn't meet his gaze and stared down at the table as if in a trance. Augusto shook his head in disappointment and disbelief, and then looked at Jada with kind but piercing eyes. "These are very serious accusations, young lady. What proof do you have?"

Jada turned to a page of the translation of the Russian merger filing document and pointed to Enrico's name with the title CEO next to it in the section entitled "New Management." She reached into her backpack and pulled out the original document in Russian so he could see Enrico's name there as well. She took out a number of documents, letters, a flash drive, and a cellphone, and placed them all in a pile in front of Augusto.

"Enrico has had a deep-seated hatred for two men for a long time. The person he detests more than anyone else is his cousin and boss, Giovanni," Jada said, turning to Giovanni. "Most of you here know that they do not have a positive working relationship." Heads nodded around the room. "Giovanni is a particularly harsh manager to his younger cousin, and it was mentioned by a number of family members in interviews with my father that this treatment was an extension of their relationship as children. In short, Giovanni bullied Enrico as a child, and bullies him as a boss." Giovanni snorted derisively at this last statement but did not deny it.

"Transfer documents we found in connection with the search for the lost scepter show that it was to be transferred to a Russian shell company. The purpose of a shell company is to shield its shareholders from public scrutiny, but Commissario Ruffalo of the Italian police department investigated the long chain of ownership, which ends with its ultimate owner, Boris Blatov. Blatov is an avid collector of artifacts and antiquities. The scepter of Maxentius was to be the crown jewel of his collection. Enrico got Blatov to pay him fifty-five million euros for the scepter, but the payment he was most interested in was being made CEO of Industria Boroni once the Blatov Group had acquired the company."

Augusto turned to Giovanni, shaking his head in disgust. "So your close personal friend Boris Blatov is nothing but a double-crosser who was going to destroy our company for profit and oust you as CEO in payment for stolen property."

"There's more," Jada continued. "Enrico arranged the international transfer of the stolen scepter through intermediaries known for smuggling stolen art and artifacts, pretending to be acting on behalf of Giovanni. I was fed clues of this transaction through messages from an unnamed 'amica' so that I would eventually uncover Giovanni as the seller of the scepter and go to the police with this information. Enrico's planned revenge was twofold. He intended to oust Giovanni as CEO and take over the position himself, as well as frame Giovanni for a major heist and send him to jail for a very long time," Jada concluded.

"*Lladrone!*" Giovanni cried and leapt out of his seat, hurling himself across the table at Enrico. Documents flew everywhere, and as if a spell had been broken, Enrico sprang into action and dashed out of the conference room door. "I will kill him," Giovanni yelled, climbing down off the table and preparing to take off after him.

"Papa, please calm down," Carlo said. "Enrico may be a thief, but he won't get away."

"Commissario Ruffalo has her officers stationed throughout the building and at every exit," Jada added. "He won't get very far. And neither will you." Jada turned to look at Maria Carla, Giovanni's assistant, who had gotten up and was standing by the coffee station near the conference room door. She had one hand on the door when Jada addressed her. "You have more than one enemy, Giovanni. Enrico wasn't working alone. He had help from the person closest to you, who knew your business dealings and your schedule inside and out, and who knew how to forge your signature perfectly. Maria Carla signed your name on the transfer documents for the scepter, which we found together with the Russian merger filing document I just showed you in a secret compartment in her desk drawer. The *amica* who sent me messages to try to frame you was none other than your assistant, Maria Carla."

Sensing the futility of trying to flee, a defiant Maria Carla tossed her hair and stared Giovanni in the eye before calmly filling her coffee cup and going to sit in a chair in a corner of the room. "She and Enrico were lovers and plotted against you together," Jada continued. Maria Carla was smart enough to admit nothing in front of a room of witnesses, but the glare of hatred in her eyes as she stared down her boss left no uncertainty as to the truth of Jada's accusations.

As assistants scrambled to put scattered papers in order, Augusto stood up and walked over to Jada. He took her hand in his and shook it warmly. "Your detective work has saved my company and purged our family of a conniving thief. Without the information you uncovered, we might have made the gravest error in the history of Industria Boroni by selling our precious business to a buyer with plans to destroy it. I cannot thank you enough, Jada."

Augusto turned and spoke sharply to his son. "Giovanni, don't you have something to say to Jada as well, since she just saved you from being implicated in a crime you did not commit?"

"*Grazie*," Giovanni said to Jada, simply but sincerely.

# CHAPTER 28

Commissario Ruffalo entered the conference room, followed by a handcuffed Enrico, flanked on either side by two uniformed officers. Two more officers entered, and at a nod from the *commissario*, went over to Maria Carla and placed her in handcuffs as well. The *commissario* shook hands with Augusto and introduced herself. "*Va bene con Lei, Signor Boroni, se parliamo in inglese?*" she asked.

"Why yes, of course, continue in English so our American guests will fully understand," Augusto graciously replied.

"Given the number of interested parties and our desire to secure a statement on the record as soon as possible, we thought we would conduct our interrogation here in your offices where everyone is already assembled. Your nephew has waived his right to an attorney," said Commissario Ruffalo.

"I have not waived any of my rights!" Maria Carla stated emphatically.

"Then we will refrain from questioning you until your lawyer is present, Signorina Morelli," responded the *commissario*. She nodded to Officer Donetti, and he placed a recording device on the conference room table.

"Signor Mattoni, may I call you Enrico?" the *commissario* asked. Enrico nodded. "Are you responsible for the theft of the scepter of Maxentius, and did you try to pin the blame for this crime on your cousin, Giovanni Boroni?"

"I did," Enrico said clearly and forcefully, "and my only regret is that I got caught. Giovanni has stolen my dignity and my rightful place in this family and this business. He is the real thief, and he deserved to be labeled as such."

"And other than Maria Carla Morelli, who else aided in your scheme?" Commissario Ruffalo asked.

"Maria Carla acted as liaison between me and Ivan Golakov, who was able to execute my plan to steal the scepter with the help of a museum guard we bribed. He was known to her as a strongman, essentially a gun for hire, because of his work for Giovanni," Enrico answered.

"What work did Ivan do for Giovanni?" the *commissario* asked.

"Intimidate me and my family!" Jada piped in before she could stop herself.

"You are correct, Jada," Enrico responded. "I knew from Maria Carla that Ivan's initial mandate from Giovanni was to try to interfere with the AmeriFoods deal by getting you and your family to leave Rome. It was Giovanni who gave the instruction to Ivan to plant the ivory in your backpack to cause you problems at the airport, and to have you robbed at the Colosseum. He also had Ivan arrange to give you and your father food poisoning in Piazza Navona, and as well sent some henchmen to menace you when you were jet skiing. Giovanni doesn't like to get his hands dirty, so he had Maria Carla handle all of his shady dealings, including instructing and paying Ivan.

"Giovanni and Ivan didn't know it, but at times, through Maria Carla, I was the one giving Ivan assignments—to steal the scepter from the museum reception and handle the logistics of its transfer to Boris Blatov in Russia through *Monsieur* Paul, a Belgian arts dealer. I had her tell Ivan that you were trying to track down the scepter and that he should stop you at all costs. He thought he was working for Giovanni and had no idea of the true source of his instructions. Like I said, Ivan was a gun for hire who did as he was told, kept his mouth shut, and didn't ask too many questions. My hope was that he would either scare you, your family, and AmeriFoods away so the company could easily be sold to Blatov, or lead you to Giovanni as the thief of the scepter. At the same time that she was instructing Ivan on the transfer of the scepter and intimidating you, she was acting as your *amica* to lead you to Giovanni as the thief."

"*Commissario*, may I?" Jada asked. The *commissario* nodded her consent, and Jada turned to Enrico. "Was Maria Carla really just a go-between between you and Ivan, or was she your partner in plotting the scheme? Did she share your ambition to run Industria Boroni once Giovanni was out of the picture?"

Enrico Mattoni looked over at Maria Carla with eyes full of anguish and something much more—*amore*. "*Basta!* Enough! I will say nothing more about Maria Carla's involvement in all of this. I take full responsibility for everything, and she is guilty only of loving me."

"How very chivalrous of you. I'm sure the fifty-five million euros Blatov was going to pay for the scepter did nothing to motivate Maria Carla," Commissario Ruffalo commented sarcastically. "Despite the huge amount you stood to receive, your primary motive for stealing the scepter was not money but revenge, and not limited to revenge against just Giovanni Boroni," she continued. "There is someone else you hate almost as much as you hate your cousin, am I right? Marco Vitti is also the subject of your ire."

"Marco Vitti is another thief who stole my work when I was an archeology student and he was my professor, then later used it to discover the scepter. He deserved to be discredited by having the scepter stolen from under his very nose!" Enrico replied passionately.

"Were you the anonymous sender of harassing and threatening letters to Vitti over the years?" Jada asked.

"Every last insult was merited," Enrico replied defiantly.

The *commissario* took a bound booklet from her briefcase and placed it on the conference room table. She explained for the record the information given in the testimony of Marco Vitti to the Sicilian police. "Marco Vitti, the assistant director of the National Museum of Rome, fled to Sicily when the burden of suffering years of harassment, combined with marital problems and being under suspicion for stealing the scepter, became too much. Ten years ago, Vitti was the leader of a panel of professors at the University of Rome who interviewed Enrico when he was a student in archeology. Enrico's thesis paper, a copy of which I have here, was on the Scepter of Maxentius. At the time, Vitti found the arguments supporting Enrico's hypothesis as to where the scepter may have been buried unpersuasive, and wrote as much in his comments failing the paper, and denying Enrico his degree. To add insult to injury, it was Vitti's team from the museum that actually found the scepter last year."

"Was Enrico correct? Was the scepter found where he earlier hypothesized it might be?" Augusto asked.

"It was found nearby, yes. Vitti suspected it was Enrico who was harassing him, but he kept quiet about it because he didn't want to admit he had used the work of Enrico's thesis to find the scepter," the *commissario* answered. "It is now clear that stealing the scepter had the added benefit to Enrico of discrediting and embarrassing Vitti."

"THIEVES!!!" Enrico shouted, jumping to his feet. Immediately the two officers at his sides clamped their hands on his shoulders and pushed him back down into his seat. "Giovanni and Marco Vitti, they are the true thieves," he cried in anguish. "And they have reduced me to becoming like them," he continued, sobbing. Enrico slumped forward and hid his face in his bound hands.

"Please pull yourself together," Commissario Ruffalo instructed Enrico. "I need you to answer the most important question of all, where is the scepter?"

But Enrico Mattoni would say no more. He refused to lift his head to respond to the *commissario*.

"I can answer that," Jada offered. "Thanks to Carlo, we were able to listen to many conversations between Enrico and Maria Carla on the Industria Boroni internal phone-tapping system. The scepter was hidden in a place where Enrico could visit it from time to time, but where, if it were discovered, the theft could still be attributable to Giovanni Boroni."

"And where is this, Jada?" the *commissario* asked.

Justin placed the cardboard box the teens had brought into the conference room onto the table and opened the top. Carlo went into Jada's backpack, pulled out a pair of green latex gloves, and handed them to Jada. She put them on and carefully reached into the box and lifted out a heavy object wrapped in silk. Jada pulled off the silk wrapping to reveal an ornate bronze staff about twenty inches in height, with an opal-colored orb attached to the top in petal-shaped prongs. The orb caught the light, and at flickering moments seemed to glow eerily. Everyone in the conference room was transfixed by the ancient scepter that had lain hidden for almost two thousand years and yet had lost none of its majestic beauty.

Scepter of Maxentius

"We found it in the basement here at Industria Boroni headquarters, in an old storage room, in this box full of reject pasta."

# CHAPTER 29

Bocca della Verita

The next morning, after a long hot bath and good night's sleep, Jada went with Carlo to his favorite spot in Rome, the courtyard of the Church of Santa Maria in Cosmedin housing the Bocca della Verita, a marble face with a gaping mouth mounted on an exterior wall of the church. "Do you know what *Bocca della Verita* means?" Carlo asked Jada.

"Well, I know the English word *verity* means truth, so I have to assume the meaning is the same in Italian," Jada responded. "But *bocca*?" she asked.

Carlo lightly touched her lips with his fingers. "Oh, of course, *bocca* means mouth," Jada responded slowly, hoping her voice did not betray the jolt his touch had given her.

"Legend has it," Carlo said, "that if someone tells a lie while his hand is in the Bocca della Verita, the jaws of the marble god will clamp shut and his hand will be bitten off! Do we dare to give it a try, Jada?"

"Sure," Jada responded. "But you go first!"

Carlo laughed and then placed his hand inside of the Bocca. "I have had the most amazing and exciting time with you, Jada Johnson, and I hope with all my heart we will meet again soon, either here in Rome or in the United States. Now your turn." Carlo's voice had become a whisper. "Put your hand inside, Jada, and tell me if you feel the same."

Jada put her right hand in the Bocca and said softly, "I have enjoyed every moment we have spent together, Carlo, and I hope with all my heart we meet up again soon." Jada wiggled her fingers to show they were still there, and Carlo took her hand inside the Bocca and braided his fingers with hers. They looked into each other's deep brown eyes. Jada closed her eyes, and Carlo leaned forward. Gently at first, then firmly, he pressed his lips to hers. Jada felt warm and fluttery, nervous and elated all at once. Neither wanted the moment to end, but they reluctantly pulled apart and smiled. "I won't say goodbye because that would be sad," Jada said. "I like the way Italians say it better. *Arrivederci*, until we see each other again."

# CHAPTER 30

The last weekend before the start of school, Jada sat at her desk in her room at home putting together a digital scrapbook of her exciting trip to Rome. Her cursor hovered over a picture of her and Carlo at the Pantheon, when the familiar sound of a FaceTime video call sounded from her laptop.

"*Commissario, buon giorno!*" Jada said when the *commissario*'s video appeared on her screen. Officer Donnetti waved at her from the background of the office.

"Good day, Jada," was the *commissario*'s smiling reply. "We miss you and your detective skills around here. Donnetti here has a lot to live up to," she said, teasing her subordinate officer and praising Jada. "Seriously, Jada," the *commissario* continued, "we have you to thank for solving the case of the stolen scepter. The scepter is back in the museum where it belongs, and thousands can see it and learn its history. I wanted to update you and let you know that Rosela came to police headquarters and turned herself in. Unless you wish to press charges, we want to provide protection for her since she has given us information on Ivan. She's an orphan, and we have placed her with a foster family who will take care of her. She is now enrolled in school for the first time."

"That's wonderful to hear, *Commissario*. I have no desire to see Rosela behind bars. I'm glad you are able to help her," Jada replied.

"My next bit of good news for you is that we found Ivan thanks to Rosela's tip. He is wanted in three different European countries for various crimes, so it is not certain where he will ultimately end up rotting in jail. But until that is determined, he and his henchmen are behind bars here in Rome. You can feel safe if you want to come back to Europe, Jada, as Ivan can no longer be a menace to you!"

"That's a relief," Jada replied. "His is one face I would like never to see again. And the others?"

"Ivan gave up *Monsieur* Paul during his interrogation, and we are awaiting his extradition to Italy from Belgium. Boris Blatov is a different story. He's a very important man in Russia, and there is no extradition treaty between Italy and Russia. Good luck getting a Russian prosecutor to go after him. I'm afraid he is untouchable. Still, I consider this a job well done. We wouldn't have tracked down any of these criminals if it weren't for you, Jada."

Jada smiled at the compliment, then asked, "What about Enrico and Maria Carla? Any news of their fate yet?"

"They are still awaiting trial, and could each face at least ten to fifteen years in prison. Enrico made a full confession, and Maria Carla has now decided to cooperate as well. We'll see if their relationship survives separate prison terms. You can probably tell me more about Giovanni. I know he is doing a year of community service for his role in intimidating you and your family, but is he still working for Industria Boroni now that it is owned by AmeriFoods?" Commissario Ruffalo asked.

"According to my dad, he is," Jada said, "but he's been demoted. His father, Augusto, remains chairman of the board of directors of the company. Anna Conti has been promoted and named CEO, so she is now Giovanni's boss. I hear she is doing a fantastic job, and sales are up already. Giovanni has been given Enrico's old job as director in charge of research and development. He's had to get used to his new office in the basement. But Carlo writes me that now that his dad has less work and less money, he's mellowed out some and is home more. They have been spending more time together and are actually enjoying getting to know one another."

"Great news, Jada. I hope you continue honing your skills as a detective, and that we see you back in Europe soon."

"You can count on it. *Sì!*"

# PHOTO ATTRIBUTIONS

Etruscan Vases, **page 16:**
Public domain

Bernini's Canopy, **page 24:**
Vatican Altar 2, Patrick Landy, known as FSU Guy at en.wikipedia, https://commons.wikimedia.org/w/index.php?search=Inside+St.+Peter%27s+Basilica&title=Special%3ASearch&go=Go&ns0=1&ns6=1&ns12=1&ns14=1&ns100=1&ns106=1#/media/File:Vatican_Altar_2.jpg, CC BY-SA 3.0 <http://creativecommons.org/licenses/by-sa/3.0/>, via Wikimedia Commons

The Sistine Chapel Ceiling, **page 25:**
Public domain

Swiss Guards, **page 26:**
Two Men of the Swiss Guard, Alexreavis, https://commons.wikimedia.org/wiki/File:Two_Men_of_the_Swiss_Guard.jpg, CC BY-SA 3.0<http://creativecommons.org/licenses/by-sa/3.0/>, via Wikimedia Commons

The Pieta, **page 29:**
Michelangelo's Pieta 5450 cropncleaned, Stanislav Traykov, https://commons.wikimedia.org/w/index.php?search=St.+Peter%27s+Rome&title=Special%3ASearch&go=Go&ns0=1&ns6=1&ns12=

1&ns14=1&ns100=1&ns106=1#/media/File:Michelangelo's_Pieta_545
0_cropncleaned_edit.jpg, CC BY-SA 3.0<http://creativecommons.org
/licenses/by-sa/3.0/>,via Wikimedia Commons

Rome Colosseum, **page 32:**
Colosseum Exterior, FoekeNoppert, https://commons.wikimedia.org/w/
index.php?search=the+Colosseum&title=Special%3ASearch&go=Go&
ns0=1&ns6=1&ns12=1&ns14=1&ns100=1&ns106=1#/media/File:
Colosseum_exterior.jpg, CC BY-SA 3.0<http://creativecommons.org/
licenses/by-sa/3.0/>,via Wikimedia Commons

Circus Maximus, **page 35:**
Public domain

Catacombs, **page 54:**
Tomb 14, St. Paul's Catacombs, Rabat, Kritzolina, https://commons.
wikimedia.org/w/index.php?title=Special:Search&limit=20&offset=
80&profile=default&search=Catacombs&advancedSearch-current=
%7B%7D&ns0=1&ns6=1&ns12=1&ns14=1&ns100=1&ns106=1#/
media/File:Tomb_14,_St._Paul's_Catacombs,_Rabat_04.jp, CC
BY-SA 4.0 <https://creativecommons.org/licenses/by-sa/4.0>, via
Wikimedia Commons

Piazza Navona, **page 72:**
Public domain

Pantheon, **page 77:**
Pantheon, Rome 2, Andrew Wales berks, uk http://www.spaceriot.
com/, https://commons.wikimedia.org/w/index.php?search=Pantheon
&title=Special%3ASearch&go=Go&ns0=1&ns6=1&ns12=1&ns14=
1&ns100=1&ns106=1#/media/File:Pantheon,_Rome_2.jpg, CC BY
2.0<https://creativecommons.org/licenses/by/2.0>, via Wikimedia
Commons

Corner of the Four Fountains Statue, **page 86:**
https://upload.wikimedia.org/wikipedia/commons/thumb/7/74/
Quattro_Fontane_-_Juno.jpg/394px-Quattro_Fontane_-_Juno.jpg

Trevi Fountain, **page 90:**
https://upload.wikimedia.org/wikipedia/commons/0/07/
Trevi_fountain_2009_2.jpg

Ponte Milvio, **page 96:**
Ponte Milvo Roma DSC00400, Gianni o O, https://commons.wiki
media.org/w/index.php?title=Special:Search&limit=20&offset=40&
profile=default&search=ponte+milvio&advancedSearch-current=%7B
%7D&ns0=1&ns6=1&ns12=1&ns14=1&ns100=1&ns106=1#/media/
File:Ponte_Milvio_Roma_DSC00400.JPG, CC BY-SA 4.0 <https://
creativecommons.org/licenses/by-sa/4.0>, via Wikimedia Commons

Scepter of Maxentius, **page 123:**
MNR, Lalupa, https://upload.wikimedia.org/wikipedia/commons/c/
ca/MNR_medagliere_-_sala_D_le_insegne_imperiali%2C_scettro_
a_calice_P1200223.jpg, CC BY-SA 4.0 <https://creativecommons.
org/licenses/by-sa/4.0>, via Wikimedia Commons

Bocca della Verita, **page 124:**
Bocca della Verita, Roughneck, https://commons.wikimedia.org/w/
index.php?search=bocca+della+verita&title=Special%3ASearch&go=
Go&ns0=1&ns6=1&ns12=1&ns14=1&ns100=1&ns106=1#/media/
File:Bocca_della_verita.jpg, CC BY-SA 3.0 <http://creativecommons.
org/licenses/by-sa/3.0/>, via Wikimedia Commons

Made in United States
Orlando, FL
30 November 2021

10913228R00082